Lockdown at Woodside

Covid-19 and the year that changed the world

This is the second book by **Allan Coleby** published by Arena Books. The author was originally from Essex, and having lived in Cambridge and Nottingham, he taught English in a variety of secondary schools and colleges in Humberside and the north Midlands. He then became a Project Manager for Pearson working in assessment and international publishing. Having had 15 Educational books and two novels published, he retired to north Norfolk.

Lockdown at Woodside

Covid-19 and the year that changed the world

_____

Allan Coleby

Arena Books

First published by Arena Books in 2021

Arena Books
6 Southgate Green
Bury St. Edmunds
IP33 2BL.

www.arenabooks.co.uk

Allan Coleby

Lockdown at Woodside *Covid-19 and the year that changed the world*

British Library cataloguing in Publication Data. A Catalogue record
for this book is available from the British Library.

ISBN 978-1-914390-05-0

BIC categories:- FA, FHP.

Cover design
by Anna Gatt

Typeset in
Times New Roman

For Ron

&

For Margaret

Both author and publisher wish to thank **Marian Lemon** for scrutinising the first draft of the text of this book for clinical accuracy. Marian is an NMC-registered nurse of wide experience in community nursing, including visiting care homes.

Chapter 1

O h, damn!' muttered Nicky Croft, as she tried to hurry along Woodside Avenue. She was fiercely annoyed with herself.

Here she was, trying to scurry along the one mile from where she lived in Chignall to Woodside Lodge, where she was due to start work today. It was twenty to two. Minutes ago, she had seen fleecy tufts of cotton-wool cloud scudding across a blue sky. She thought she could get to the Lodge without a coat.

Now, the air cooled and the sky darkened. Dry, dead leaves swirled in little spirals that moved along the street. Soft raindrops fell onto the loose-fitting jumper that covered her blouse. She broke into a trot, glad that her skirt was not tight and that her shoes were flat.

The drops became rods of water that drove down and soaked her clothes. She felt cold. In desperation, she ran on. The sky became granite. The feeling in the air was frightening, and then a bolt of lightning split the sky. Two seconds later, the thunder thudded and rolled. The world seemed full of menace. Then suddenly, there was the large, welcoming door of the Lodge on her left.

Nicky sprinted along the short path, leapt up the three stone slabs to the shelter of the portico, pressed the bell and stood, gulping the air. She felt dreadful. What must she look like? Her first shift!

'Hello! It's Nicky, isn't it?' And in spite of everything, there was a broad, beaming smile. What a start, but what a welcome.

'Yes. Sorry to look like a drowned rat. Mrs Holden?'

'Miss Holden, yes, but call me Stella. Come in, come in. Let's get you into some dry clothes, and then we can sort you out.'

The smile did not lose its warmth. Nicky was so glad. She stumbled through the doorway, dropped her carrier bag, and shuddered with relief.

'Sorry to have to come bursting in like this, Miss Holden. I thought I had time to get here in the dry, and now look.'

'Oh, never mind about that.' Stella's voice was reassuring, too. 'Come on. Follow me up these stairs and we'll find something for you.'

Opposite the large, heavy front door through which Nicky had just come, there was spacious hallway, and then a wide, carpeted staircase with easy, shallow steps which led up to the first floor. Leading straight off the landing at the top was the door to the office and medication room. Nicky had come for her interview there, and because Stella always used it for receiving visitors and business callers or other professionals like the local GP, it had direct access from the front door. In that way, the residents were not disturbed.

As she followed now, Nicky was surprised at the speed and agility with which Stella climbed the stairs. At her interview, she had estimated her age at the late fifties, but she certainly whizzed along now. She pushed open the door, spun round and gestured for Nicky to occupy one of the easy chairs to the right. The left side of the room as she entered was filled by two large desks, one with a laptop computer, a keyboard and a separate, large screen, and a printer. The other desk was partly covered with a drawer-file, that had been left open on it, and wire trays containing letters and other documents. A two-seater settee and three easy chairs were to the right. The chairs were not the sort you might lean right back and relax in, but firmly upholstered in an upright position, and with wooden legs holding the seat at some height from the floor.

'You may remember that we have a family-sized bathroom up here,' said Stella. 'It's practically my own bathroom, because the other two bed-sits up here are usually not occupied, and when they are, the person is staying only temporarily.' Without further explanation, she rushed on: 'We've got plenty of dry towels and even some spare clothes in there, so we'll get you dry and freshly dressed before anything else.'

Without waiting for a reply, she was back out of the door, which shut quickly with a strong closer. Nicky could hear her rummaging in the bathroom next door; she sat where Stella had indicated, and put her hand to her wet hair. Stella's obviously full of a driving energy in the middle of the day, she thought, and she was really impressed by how her first concern had been to look after her new employee, in view of the bustling distress of her arrival. She had not sent Nicky to find dry clothes, but dived into the bathroom to search for them herself. No ceremony there, thought Nicky.

Stella soon reappeared, carrying a large, thick, beige jumper, a smart-looking pair of pale blue slacks and a plain blue blouse. It looked as if she had got the size right first time, thought Nicky, except for the jumper. It was very large, but the weather had suddenly turned rather cold for the beginning of March, and so she would be glad of something to snuggle into. She had brought in her carrier-bag a pair of soft shoes for inside the house, so it looked as if she would be alright.

'Here we are, then,' said Stella breezily, and still wearing a smile. 'Go back into the bathroom to change if you like, and if you leave your wet things in the bath, I'll get them done in the drier in the laundry room before you go home. I won't do any tea now, because we all have one about the middle of the afternoon. I'll explain when you've changed.'

Returning as wide a smile as she could muster, Nicky skipped round to the bathroom. 'See you in a mo,' she called. She couldn't quite bring herself to use the manager's Christian name – not yet, anyway.

Stella had picked up a letter from the desk and was scanning through it, but she put it straight down when Nicky returned. 'Oh, you look fine, Nicky. That jumper looks really comfy.' She had noticed the snuggling movements from the young teenager. 'Come on. I want to show you round this place before you start.' She made for the door, and a quick movement of the hand showed that Nicky should follow.

Then, at the door, Stella stopped and looked into Nicky's face again. 'Let's just sit down for a minute and I'll explain something about what you are likely to see.' They sat on the two chairs closest to the door. 'You'll be working shifts, you know. It's Monday the second of March today, and there's a reason why I wanted you to start on the two-to-nine shift on a Monday. It's the quietest time of the week. All afternoons are quiet, because we've got breakfast and lunch done, and all the medical things attended to on the six-to-two shift each morning. Hopefully, beds have been made and furniture put in place as well. A bit of work on the furniture and some cleaning in each room may be left over until after two, but what I've told you is the theory, anyway. Then we always have an activity provided and encouraged during the afternoons to keep people active as far as possible.

'Monday afternoon is jigsaws. You'd be surprised how popular jigsaws are. Our people here love them. They get absorbed in them, and you always have to interrupt them when it's cup-of-tea time or evening meal time. Then they'll move it carefully over to the side so that they can resume it later and go back to it sometime in the week that's convenient for them. Half one side of the laundry lounge always has part-finished jigsaws standing on small card-tables for the rest of the week, and there's such a row if someone knocks into one, or disturbs it in any way. You'll see,' said Stella, with a raising of the eyebrows intended to show there was something confidential between them. Nicky then followed Stella as she stood up from the chair, went into the bathroom, grabbed Nicky's wet clothes from the bath, and then turned back out again.

As they came out onto the landing, she continued talking. 'By the way, you'll notice that I said "laundry lounge". Well, the layout of the main house here is pretty simple. As you enter by the front door, there is a large lounge on either side of you. That on the left has the television continuously on for those who want it, and that on the right, where there is no television, is where the afternoon activity is provided, for those who want it. Those rooms were the reception rooms when this was a private house owned by my parents. Instead of calling them "left" and "right", which could be confusing, that on the right as you come in the door is known as the "laundry lounge", simply because the laundry room, the utility room in the original house, is behind it. The one on the left is the "kitchen lounge" because the kitchen and dining room are behind that. Come on, then, Nicky. Let's go down and round.'

After a steady descent of the staircase, they turned to their left and went through an open doorway to where the jigsaw-solving was taking place. Quiet concentration was the order of the day. Two tables had a couple seated at each end of them, and then there were four tables for two, where the absorption was by solitary players.

'The tables are brought through from the dining room after lunch on Mondays,' explained Stella, as they made their way through the tables to a door at the back. She did not want to interrupt the concentration with introductions to Nicky as they passed through. Obviously, that could wait until later. They could faintly hear the sound of a television set coming from the "kitchen lounge", but did not go in there: Stella wanted to press on.

At the back of the room, they went through a door directly into the laundry. It felt warm and steamy. Someone was just closing the door of one of the washing machines, having just loaded it.

'Ah, Maggie! Getting things moving, I see,' called Stella. Maggie did not look up until she had finished the programming and they could hear the soft hiss of the water entering the machine. 'This is Nicky,' Stella told Maggie as she got up from her crouch. Nicky was surprised to see how tall she was as she rose to her full height. She looked down slightly on both the other ladies as she smiled her greeting. Her dark hair was falling over her face, and she was forced to push wisps of it out of her eyes. 'I've been telling people she's coming,' continued Stella, 'and she's starting the two o' clock shift this afternoon, so you'll see more of her.'

'Glad to meet you, Nicky,' said Maggie, who was very full in the face, and had a happy, beaming smile, once she had finished adjusting her hair. 'We can certainly do with you here. We can do with all the help we can get.'

'Maggie starts at two today as well,' explained Stella, turning back to Nicky. 'Apart from washing, drying and ironing everything in sight, she's in charge of all our cleaning products and machines. They are all stored in that large cupboard, as big as a pantry, on the far wall.' She turned back to Maggie. 'We're going round the rooms now, Maggie, to introduce Nicky, see how things are and who's staying in their room today. It might only be Ella and Barbara: Ella won't know what day of the week it is, and Barbara will be reading and moaning about how painful her arthritis is, which is why she's staying in and reading. You'll see, Nicky.' She turned to her in further explanation. 'The laundry lounge is also supposed to be for people who want some peace and quiet to just sit and read the newspapers or a book or talk quietly if they can't be bothered with the TV. I'll tell you what, Maggie, you stay in here, and we'll give the rooms a bit of attention if they need it, and we'll tell you of any problems at cup-of-tea time. In fact, why don't you go up to the office and have your tea with me and Nicky this afternoon?'

'OK, Stella. I'll do that. See you later,' and she turned back to empty one of the other washing machines.

'Oh, nearly forgot,' said Stella. 'Here are Nicky's wet things. She got caught in a very heavy shower on the way here today. Could you get them dried before she finishes tonight? She's in some of our emergency garb at the moment.'

'Sure. Just leave it there.'

'Come on, Nicky. Let's go and look at the rooms.'

Stella grabbed a sweeping brush and a dustpan-with-short-brush as they went out of the back entrance of the laundry. There was a short corridor in front of them, and a large door to the right. This was not only a back entrance and exit for the laundry, but a tradesmen's entrance for provisions and services. The staff used it as a way out quite frequently. Nicky held out her hands for the dustpan and brush, and Stella gave them with a smile.

After the few yards along the short corridor, in front of Stella and Nicky there was a right-angle turn left into a long straight corridor, off which led the doors to the single, private rooms occupied by the residents. There was a name on each door, and in each room was a single bed, a two-seater settee, and a further easy chair. Along one side of the room were a direct-line landline telephone, a TV set with a recorder and DVD player, a separate radio, wi-fi provision, a table and chair suitable for a small meal or for writing or practical activities. On the other side, a small cupboard and a wardrobe stood next to a door which led into an en-suite toilet, shower and washbasin.

'We often refer to these rooms as "units", Nicky, because that is essentially what they are, an individual provision for absolute privacy, with one good-sized window to the outside. Perhaps I should also point out to you that we refer to the people who are under our care here as "guests". I don't like the word "residents" because it sounds as if we are a hotel, and we are much more than a hotel. The word "clients" makes it sound as if we are solicitors wanting to make money out of them, and they are not "patients" because they are not seriously ill, though some require regular medical care and attention. In fact, we are a residential care home "with nursing", so "guests" it is.'

Nicky's mother had told her there were different types of care home, and so she made a mental note that she would ask Stella about this later. It looked as if she would be drinking her afternoon tea with Stella, as she had twice referred to it.

Nicky could see that this long corridor reached across the back of the original house and a bit further. A glance through an outside window also showed that another similar length of the same kind of "units" went at right angles from the end of the corridor, so that there was a large L-shaped arrangement of buildings which enclosed a car park and then, further on, the lawns of a well-tended garden.

'This is Vic's room,' said Stella, as they came across the first door on the left. She took a large bunch of keys, deftly selected one, turned it in the lock and pushed it open so that they could both advance a step or two and look round. 'Oh, this will be OK,' she said. 'He's obviously made his bed and tidied round everywhere. Most of the guests do, and we don't always need to use these brushes and dusters. I haven't brought either the large or small vacuum cleaner, so we'll just leave this room as it is, and press on. You'll notice there's a small panel to the right of each door that lights up to say "Do not disturb" if they don't want us in at all, for whatever reason. And by the head of each bed there is also a button that they can push that rings a bell in the office or activates my pager or that of any other nurse on duty if they ever need any urgent attention at any time, day or night.

'Don't ever mention sport, or ask what he did in his earlier life,' said Stella light-heartedly, as they approached the next door. 'Apparently, he was a good cricketer, and achieved different things in football as well, and he just loves to talk about it all to anyone who'll listen. So don't ask, unless you want to be delayed for half an hour and stopped from getting on with anything else.

'This one's Jane's,' Stella continued, as they unlocked and entered the next room. 'She's a lovely lady, always thinking of other people and wanting to know if she can help in any way. Yes, it's always scrupulously tidy,' she said, as she looked round. There was a used cup of tea on the table with some dregs in the bottom, so Stella took it, emptied it down the sink in the en-suite and dried it with a tea-towel on a rack underneath. 'There's an old film on the TV this afternoon in the kitchen lounge, so I expect Jane's watching it in there. She loves them.'

'I'd better shut up about who's who for now, Nicky,' said Stella. 'You'll soon learn who everyone is, and their different characters. We'd better bash on if we're going to make a few changes to these rooms, get back into the office by half-past three and let Maggie know what else needs doing, especially the vacuuming.'

Nicky had brought a tray with cups, saucers, milk and a pot of tea with another small pot of hot water up to the office at 3.30. Stella had shown her round the kitchen and where to get provisions for herself and the guests. Sam Wild, the chef, was the only cook and he, Stella said, worked every morning seven days a week from 6am until 2pm. This covered all breakfasts and all lunches. Over time, she explained, Woodside care home had developed the practice of making lunch, 12.30 until 2pm, the main meal of the day. A number of factors made this the best thing: afternoon activities, such as bus trips out, shopping, entertainments, could then occur during the main part of the day. Many guests did not like to eat substantially during the late afternoon or evening, and so it suited everyone's digestion and activity plans. Therefore, tea or coffee, milk, sugar, cakes and biscuits could easily be fetched for guests by the carer on duty during the mid-afternoon break, and Sam left a choice of snack meals ready-prepared in the kitchen for the carer to serve in the dining room or in the units in the early evening. Choice of the snack meal and whether they would be in the dining room or their unit was made by the guests after breakfast each morning. Choice of lunch was also made at that time.

Nicky and Stella had found, as they went round, that three of the guests were staying in for the afternoon: Martin, Ella and Barbara. By a coincidence, they were all in the middle of the first corridor: Martin in Room 4, Ella and Barbara in Rooms 5 and 6. Maggie arrived just in time to take tea, coffee and cakes into the laundry lounge for the jigsaw people, and, while Stella went off to serve the TV-watchers, Nicky took the refreshments to Martin, Ella and Barbara in their rooms. She thought she could introduce herself, and see whether they remembered her name from when she called an hour ago.

'Don't worry too much about Ella,' said Stella. 'Just tell her the tea is rather hot at the moment. She'll forget your name again, anyway. Don't let Martin get talking to you. Make it quick. See you in the office in a few minutes.'

'How did you find those who had stayed in their rooms, Nicky?' asked Stella as she, Nicky and Maggie sat down in the office and started drinking their tea.

'Ella seemed to be just staring ahead and doing nothing,' was Nicky's reply, 'but I asked her if she was OK and suggested she wiped her nose. She just nodded and blew her nose. Barbara was reading and complaining that she couldn't get comfortable because her arthritis was hurting. And Martin – oh, no! In the end I just looked at my watch, said "Just look at the time" and walked out. You might like to know that the Covid-19 virus is advancing like a menacing army across Europe and will soon be here – that's Martin's advice, anyway.'

'Always full of happy news,' Stella commented. 'Jigsaws OK, Maggie?' Maggie nodded.

'Righto. Well, Nicky, you've looked inside all the rooms now except the dining room. That's a pleasure you can share with me at six tonight. Maggie, those delightful, lazy, untidy men, Lew, Mick and Chris, in "Sportsmen's corner" down there, 9,10 and 11: their rooms looked like the inside of a waste bin, but Nicky and I tidied them. Could you run the vacuum cleaner round them? Then, don't bother with the dining room tonight – Nicky and I will see to it. When you've cleaned the floor and wound the laundry down for today, just go home when you're ready.'

'Thanks, Stella,' replied Maggie. 'I could do with getting off early tonight. It's been the usual sleepy Monday.'

There was a pause while the three of them sipped their tea and started on the slices of lemon cake and one or two of the delightful cup-cakes that Sam had left ready for them that day. Nicky felt the sense of easy familiarity. They were all happy to nibble away at the cake and share the silence without feeling that they had to fill the silence with talk.

Nicky glanced round the room again. They were sitting in the easy chairs on one side of it. Opposite, the computer desk was much as it had been earlier: the laptop, screen, keyboard and printer. The drawer-file had been removed and the surface was clear, though the wire baskets were brimming with untidy papers, probably correspondence, and official-looking booklets and brochures. No doubt, she thought, this place is always being bombarded with regulations, guidance and updates from the County Council and the Government departments of Health and Social Services.

'Now, I was telling you earlier about the type of care home we are,' Stella resumed the conversation. 'We are an average kind of care home, neither a hotel nor a hospital, about in the middle of the scale of how much the staff have to help the residents with the routines of everyday living, such as washing, dressing, eating, bathing or showering, taking them to the toilet and taking their regular medication, because almost all of them have to rely on something. We are certainly not a nursing home, the kind of place that provides palliative and end-of-life care. We do not give specialist support of life-limiting illness with the clinical needs of the relief of symptoms of pain and sickness. There may also be in nursing homes people who need specialist emotional and spiritual support. We do, though, have guests who need vigilant medical care, and I think I told you at your interview, we have two fully qualified nurses on our staff, Jo and Kath. Each of them has a degree and are NMC registered. I also am qualified in that respect and NMC registered, though I don't have a degree because in my day, it was more a matter of specialism courses and on-the-job training.

'This means that medically we are well-covered, and we do offer respite care, where we have for a week or up to a month, guests who are quite ill because their condition has deteriorated to a critical level, but whose regular carers need a short break or a holiday. We don't have permanent guests with complex medical needs, but with respite care you never know quite who you are going to get. I always accommodate them in the two larger rooms on this first floor the other side of the bathroom. I can keep an eye on them there.

'We also have what is called intermediate care provision. This is for people who have finished with the specific treatment the hospital provides for recovery from their medical condition or from surgery, but may be in need of further help, for instance from a physiotherapist, before they go home. So they will be moved to us from the local Brookfields hospital to prevent bed-blocking. The hospital is especially keen on that at the moment because there seems to be a new virus spreading from the East and they don't know how full they are going to be.

'So you see, Nicky, that whereas we do have palliative and respite provision with three fully qualified nurses, if you include me, we are mostly a middle-of-the-road residential care home with nursing. Each guest has a personalised care plan, with everything from medical needs to more general life-interests. We have on-site facilities such as hairdressing and a small library, with the local library van calling regularly. Occasionally, we have days out visiting National Trust properties, eating lunch out somewhere, or going to markets in nearby towns. We also do jigsaws, board games, gentle indoor party games, a music-and-movement session, and even sometimes a local entertainer with jokes and monologues who brings along his keyboard for a good-humoured community singalong. It all helps the general health and well-being of our guests and is even fun for the staff, too.'

'Wow, that's quite an advert for your care home, Stella,' said Nicky.

'Well, I wanted to give you a balanced picture of our life here,' said Stella. 'It's not all doom and gloom, but it's fun with a lot of variety as well. I live here all the time, with my bedroom, sitting room and bathroom up here on the first floor. This is because I am totally committed here. I have made this place my life. My parents owned the original large house here, and as I was their only child, they were bound to leave it to me. I had been a hospital nurse when I was a young lady, but I left that job to nurse both my parents in their old age. By the time that was finished, I was well past the marrying age, so I devoted myself to Woodside Lodge. My parents left me a very large sum of money and other assets, and so I had the house modified to be a care home. I had those two wings of nine units each on the ground floor purpose-built so that each unit can be a self-contained home for each occupant. Of course, we all need the communal kitchen and dining room, though guests can eat in their own rooms if they want to.

'Is there anything you want to ask me, Nicky, before I go on again and explain a bit more? Oh, by the way, I should have told you this before, but your DBS check was fine, so there's no need to worry there.' And Stella smiled again – that broad, friendly, reassuring smile that Nicky saw when she first entered through the front door.

Stella turned to Maggie: 'You go if you want, Maggie, as soon as you have finished those rooms, Lew, Mick and Chris's. Nicky and I will serve all the evening meals tonight. You're on at two again tomorrow, aren't you?' As soon as Maggie had quickly agreed and gone out, Stella continued: 'Oh, she's a wonderful worker, Nicky. She's a tower of strength. I don't know where she gets her energy from, but she really keeps this place going with her hard work.'

'And she's so friendly with it,' said Nicky.

'Yes,' Stella nodded. 'Now, I'm sure you have lots of things you want to ask me.' Then came the broad smile. 'You get paid on the last Thursday of each month, with a cheque, together with a payslip showing all deductions, in case that's the first thing you're going to ask.'

'Well, thank you. But you have already told me about the first thing I wondered, which was what kind of care home we are. I know now, "a residential care home, with nursing", as you said. Will I have to administer any medicines to the residents?'

'Guests,' corrected Stella with a smile. 'Always remember, Nicky, that those in our care do not live in our work-place; we serve and support them in their home. The answer to your question is, "No". As I told you, including me, we have three well-qualified and experienced nurses here, and although neither of the other two work here in the afternoon, they have agreed to be on call in case of an emergency and I am always here day and night, except when I'm doing my personal shopping or any other business. What we need you for, Nicky, is basic caring duties: personal attention to the guests who need you in respect of washing and showering, eating and drinking, organising their rooms, going to the toilet, walking around the house or garden or going into the nearby village if that is planned; everyday tasks like cleaning, organising their laundry and managing their money; serving meals at breakfast, lunch and evening snacks; assisting with any activities arranged for the afternoon in the lounges or on any trips out; and, above all, just being friendly, making them happy, arranging contact with families, developing friendships, helping with their hobbies and assisting with their physical exercise if they do any. It is as well regularly to consult their "personal care plan" kept in the office, to make sure that we are keeping up with everything they need. After all, either they are paying, or the social services department of the Council is paying for them, or sometimes an insurance company, so we must take care to fulfil the contract, though always with a smile if possible.' Stella concluded with one of her glowing smiles. 'Now that's enough to be going on with, isn't it?'

'I can't wait to get started,' said Nicky, collecting the rest of the tea things onto a tray that Maggie had left behind.

'You have started,' was Stella's comment. 'You've been in all the private units with me, met three of the guests, seen the laundry and found your way round the kitchen. Although your shifts don't coincide this week, I'm sure you'll see Sam, the chef, at some time soon. He works from six until two seven days a week, but has one week in seven off. Then, we have a relief chef. You've met Maggie and I've told you about Kath Taylor and Jo Rayner, the nurses. Could I just say that, although we need them for their medical knowledge, Kath and Jo join in with the general domestic and caring duties during their shift. It's just that health, medicine and prescription drugs are their priority; after that, they muck in in the mornings, which is when they're on. You'll soon meet Linda Doyle and Laura

Kemp, the two other full-time carers, young women who are strong and competent enough for the job. So with you and Sam Wild, the chef, that makes eight of us, including me.

'Anyway, Maggie's finishing the cleaning and laundry at the moment, and what we have to do is look into the lounges to make sure everything is alright, and then go and sort out the dishes Sam has left for the light evening meal. Come on, let's go.'

'Oh, by the way,' Stella turned back to Nicky as they got out onto the landing in front of the office again, 'on most afternoons at this time, you will see visitors. They come in and drift around the place looking for their particular relative if they have not told them they're coming, or they can't find them in their private room. But there are very few, usually none on Mondays, so I don't expect we'll see any today. They are welcome to come in at any time, but they hardly ever come in the mornings. It is always the afternoons, usually towards the end of the week, and especially on Sundays. On Sunday afternoons, we get a bit overwhelmed sometimes. If they're here at cup-of-tea time and are in a lounge, offer them tea and a bit of cake, and you must be very friendly. After all, it's they who are paying usually. Come on, then.' She hardly paused for breath, and didn't expect a reply as she started down the stairs. 'Let's wander round the lounges for a few minutes before we get to the food.'

A quiet concentration filled the laundry lounge with the jigsaw people, and in the kitchen lounge, the film had obviously finished and the viewers were casually watching one of the 'Reality TV' auctions which seemed to be broadcast so often. One of the men, Maurice, was sitting in one of the armchairs reading. Many of the TV-watchers seemed to be dozing in their chairs. After a short time, Stella and Nicky went through the back door into the dining room.

'Now the first thing we have to do, Nicky, is to set the tables before we go through into the kitchen,' Stella began. 'The people who want to come and eat their evening meal in here, which is almost all of them, should have shown that by ticking a list on that clipboard on the small table over by the door. I looked earlier and fifteen people will be coming in here tonight. Quite often, people have forgotten to fill in the list, and just turn up, but I should think fifteen will be right for tonight, so we'll take the meals for the other three on trays to their rooms. They don't very often make a mistake the other way round, tick for in here, and then stay in their rooms.' She shrugged. 'Right. So, the first thing is to make sure there are placemats for fifteen and then put a set of cutlery in each place. We'll set two tables for four and then four tables for two. That's a spare set for anyone who's forgotten. It's never quite right, but the guests will re-arrange themselves as they want when they come in. We try to start at 5.30. We just start and do it, and if anyone is late and the soup starts to cool, it's their hard luck.

'There's always soup, by the way. The rest of the evening snack is cold, because the carers, including me, don't cook. The only hot food we prepare is the soup. Sam has left it ready, and we switch it on about quarter past five and keep it going in a large tub with a slow burner. Everyone has had a hot meal at lunchtime, but if people need warming later, there's the soup. Then there's what ever Sam has provided for that day. There's one of his specialities tonight: sliced cold Bakewell tart. He seems to like doing that, because we get it quite often. And there's always a bread-and-butter or buttered toast addition if anyone wants, but they have to ask, and a cup of tea afterwards as well. So let's put the soup spoons, knives and forks ready and then we'll get into the kitchen.

'It's Sid, Christine and June, 14, 16 and 17 on the far corridor, who have decided to stay in their rooms tonight, so can I leave them to you, Nicky?' She continued, and went straight on without waiting for an answer. 'Can you look in on Ella in No. 5 and ask her, too, because she probably won't turn up because she's forgotten?'

'Fine, Stella,' said Nicky, using her name for the first time. She got a smile from Stella, as they went into the very large, spacious kitchen. 'By the way, you'll see there's another door out of the kitchen which leads along to the first corridor. You don't have to go out and through the lounges to get there, and I'll just tell you some of the procedures before you start picking them up from me,' she went on, squatting down on a small stool in the corner.

'We serve everything to the guests, breakfast, lunch and tea. We can't have the guests walking about and carrying food and drink. Many of them have walking sticks that they have to bring in with them, anyway, and if they helped themselves, there would be spillages, and falls, and any other kind of accident. You can see that we've got a maximum of six tables in here tonight, and there are two of us after you've seen to those in the far corridor, so we'll be OK. The guests don't often ask for bread and butter or toast after Sam's snack. With the tea afterwards, there are pots of tea for two, which we make in the kitchen and then bring it in here, one pot for a table of two, two for a table of four. And the sugar and milk is never out beforehand: we bring it in from the kitchen with the teapots.'

Stella could tell that Nicky was following all these simple instructions, which would soon become automatic for her, and so she started pulling teapots, cups, sugar bowls and small milk jugs from the deep shelves on the back wall.

The large clock on the back wall showed it was twenty past five, and so Stella said, 'Let's make a start.' She opened three large, glass-fronted chilled containers, rather like those in supermarkets, and took out large plates on which were portions of the cold Bakewell tart that Sam had left prepared. She took off the light covering and set them all on the side by the outside wall. 'You can keep the covering on the small ones and start taking them on trays with cutlery to Sid, Christine and June if you like, and I'll wait for the first guests to start wandering into the dining room and present them with their plates once they've sorted out who's sitting with who. Then I'll serve the soup.'

For the next hour, Nicky didn't stop, going back and forth to the far corridor, in the sequence Stella had described, and she tried to concentrate on the same two tables for two, while Stella attended to the rest. It all went smoothly. She could see why the guests in the rooms wanted to be there: they wanted to keep their eyes on the television while they ate. One of her tables asked for toast, and she made it for them while their tea was cooling.

In no time at all it was seven-thirty, and Nicky joined Stella washing up in the large sink and drainer. The few cups and plates were hardly soiled at all and there was no grease or stickiness, so it was quicker to do things by hand than it was to load up two of the dishwashers. The two women ate left-over sections as they worked.

'There's always enough left over for us,' said Stella, 'at breakfast and lunch as well. It means we eat on the go, but it means you don't need to bring any pack-up with you.'

The guests slowly wandered off to the lounges, or to their rooms to spend a short evening and prepare for bed.

Nicky realised she felt a little tired now that her shift was ending, but she was quite elated. She had got the first day over, without any mishaps, and it all seemed to be going well.

Nurse Jo Rayner arrived to do the night shift at nine. Nicky was impressed when she gave her a smile really exuding genuine warmth, as Stella introduced her. She had fair hair with a parting on the left so that her hair swept down on either side of her forehead and came to an end just below her ears – no fuss, but neat, strong and well-controlled. Her broad, conventional-looking face complemented a wide, good-natured looking mouth with very pale lipstick matching a very pale eye-shadow. This attractive appearance, along with her confident manner, evoked an equally warm response from Nicky. Something in her straight back and authoritative bearing made Nicky decide that here was an experienced nurse who would take control of any situation and be relied on to make sound and effective decisions.

'I hope you'll be happy here, Nicky,' she said with an equally calm and reassuring tone of voice. 'You've finished your first day and you're on your way home now?'

'Yes,' breathed Nicky. 'I'm pleased to meet you, Jo.'

With that, Nicky went into the laundry to find her dry clothes that Maggie had left for her, went to the upstairs bathroom to change and then grabbed the bag she had brought with her. She changed into her outdoor shoes, and with a wave and a smile towards Stella, she went downstairs again and into Woodside Avenue. She was very happy.

Chapter 2

John Croft, Nicky's father, looked at the body of a young girl lying partly concealed by the undergrowth in the wood. She was fully clothed, but her clothes were torn and roughly pulled about.

Then he glanced at his watch. Six-thirty. Well, the police had wasted no time in getting him and his employer, Jim Borrett, out to this corpse early in the morning. Unless there were any problems, they would soon have the poor girl into the morgue and he would be back home in time for breakfast with his family.

John worked part-time for Jim, an undertaker based in John's home village of Chignall. His main job was as a salesman for Anscombe's, a well-known manufacturer of electric fires. He travelled all over the country visiting retailers from September to February each winter, selling a range of different models of fire. But from March to August, he worked flexi-time, doing administration and as a holiday relief worker. This meant he could organise his own time and, paid by the job, could work part-time for his friend, Jim.

This scene was typical of the work John did. It was the nasty, unpleasant side of being an undertaker, something Jim's regular workers would rather not do, if he could find someone else. People often died early in the morning, elderly people during their first visit to the toilet, or they might be found in bed when it was too late to attempt to revive them. Once a doctor had come and confirmed that death had occurred, if an ambulance that had been called could not take them, the police called Jim Borrett with his black Transit van. In small letters, at the bottom of the door, were the words "James Borrett – private ambulance", but everyone knew that was a euphemism for "body van". Occasionally, a body would be found in a derelict building during the night and then, once a doctor had been and gone, a policeman would have to wait for Jim and an assistant, to make sure the right person was taking it away. These were the most unpleasant corpses of all, often not solid or dry. They would need a plastic body-bag and two men to manipulate it. The smell could be overpowering. This one, though, was fairly accessible and not too heavy. A dog walker, in the really early morning, as dawn was breaking, went to investigate why his dog would not return to him, and he had his phone with him to call the police.

'How long do you think she's been gone?' John asked Jim, who was very experienced in these matters.

'I should think the pathologist will decide she died in the late evening, last night,' he replied. 'Careful, careful,' he added, as John stumbled over a root and the body slipped along the heavy, strong stretcher. He caught the weight with his gloved hand and pushed it back. 'The jaw and neck were pretty stiff and the arms were rigid, but the joints are not too solidly locked yet. When I first pulled the head round, the skin was cold enough,' he continued as they carefully took the load through the back doors and slid it slowly along the runners into position. 'That purplish-grey colour is about right for a few hours,' he added. 'It will go more blue-grey later.' He closed the doors gently, and then turned away, glad to escape the sickly-sweet smell as he walked along the side of the van and clambered into the cab, knocking mud off his boots on the running board as he did so.

'And what happened to the poor girl?' asked John, as he climbed in the opposite door.

'Well, you saw the marks on the neck, and the eyes were still open when we got there,' said Jim. 'This must be murder, and it looks to me like strangulation.'

'Lovers' quarrel?'

'Drugs, more like.'

Little was said for the rest of the journey, each man content with his own thoughts. The early morning was always the quietest, calmest time of the day, before traffic built up to slow things down. Once they got to Gainsford, they drove round to the back of Brookfields hospital and parked to unload at the Pathology department.

After a quiet drive back to Chignall, it was still only just after eight when Jim dropped John off outside his house, and he went inside to have a good wash and to join his family at breakfast. He could hear that they were seated round the table in the dining room, but there was no smell of bacon or frying eggs, and so they were obviously making do with cereals. The talk stopped as he entered the room.

'Been a bad one, Dad?' asked Sean, who was seventeen, just over a year younger than Nicky. He was in Year twelve at the local comprehensive.

'A bit sad and grizzly, yeah,' John replied, 'especially because it was a young girl and it had been violent,' he added. No-one spoke.

The quiet persisted.

'What shift are you on today, love?' John asked Yvonne, who was middle-aged like himself and who had some sort of supervisory job at the Co-op supermarket in Chignall, which was a large village of some 4,000 inhabitants.

'I'm not on until two today,' she said, 'but that means I won't be back until well after ten tonight.'

'You and Nicky both,' said John. 'I'm beginning to think that the women do the work in this house,' he said, in good humour.

'I couldn't do what you've just done,' said Yvonne. 'You're going into the care industry now, Nicky,' she said, and then, after a pause: 'Oh, I do hope you don't see too much of the really rough side of it for a while.' She looked steadily at her daughter with compassion, and not a little admiration for the decision she had made.

'Well, it's what I've decided to do with my life at present,' said Nicky. 'It's better than those two years I spent at Debenham's. I never had any sense of looking after anyone. Some of the customers treated you like dirt. I think I may move properly into nursing eventually,' she said calmly, and a little dreamily.

'In that case you'll need a degree eventually,' said Sean, 'and I think you'd be better studying it full-time, so that you can achieve it faster,' he said.

'No,' countered Nicky. 'I'm restless unless I'm doing things. I like helping people, more than anything. I'm a practical person.'

'Well, anyway, I'm really interested in my Science at the moment, and in the end I'm aiming to be a bio-chemist of some sort.'

'What about a doctor, then?'

'No. I'm not such a "people person" as you are.'

Nicky shrugged. 'Each to his own,' she said, getting up from the table. She had finished, and began to take off the dishes to wash them.

'Oh, Nicky, I'm sorry,' said Stella at two o' clock that day, after Nicky had run up the central staircase and bounced into the office where Stella was just turning away from the desk. 'I didn't tell you yesterday, but we've got one of our "outing" days today. They're always on a Tuesday, which is usually not too busy, before the crowds build up towards the weekend in the summer at least, and it starts to get that way in Spring, although we are only at the beginning of March at the moment. They are just days out in our minibus, to a nearby town with a good shopping centre, or a market on a Tuesday, or we might visit an ancient monument or a National Trust property, or get as far as the coast in the summer. It's only a small minibus, specially adapted to take two wheelchairs through a very wide rear door if we want, and there's a small, special flight of steps that comes down to the pavement to help those who can't walk much to get up into the seats. It's always big enough because only half or less of the guests ever want to go. Depending on where we go, it can be a bit costly because they have to pay extra for it, you see. We hire a driver, a chap in the village who has a PSV licence.'

Stella paused for a deep intake of breath. 'Anyway, today they've gone to Stamford for lunch and a trip round Rutland water this afternoon. There's a sight-seeing boat that starts trips in March, but we phoned the people who run it this morning, and they say it's a bit chilly and the water's a bit choppy today, so they've cancelled. So our people are going for a ride round the reservoir in the bus. There's a tea-room they can stop at in Whitwell, by the side of Rutland water, before they come home, and that will be all they'll want. There'll be cream teas later on in the summer, but I don't think they'll have started them yet.'

There was another pause and a smile. 'Maggie's gone with them,' she continued. 'It's usually Maggie that goes. She spends so much of her time in that hot, steamy laundry, and on top of that, she's Mrs Mop for the building, so I feel she deserves to get out and enjoy herself with the guests when there's a chance to do so. If we need any of the washing machines in the laundry today, I'll go and do it, and I'll get out the mops and vacuum cleaners and brushes for anyone who needs them for the lounges or the corridors.

'Linda Doyle is starting the two-till-nine shift today and she'll be on it all week. You haven't met her yet, but I'm sure you two will get along fine. If you could, between you, keep an eye on both lounges, all the rooms in both corridors and the dining room at five-thirty, Nicky, that will be fine.

'Those on the trip will be back at about four, so they'll want the evening snack along with everyone else, but don't expect them to be there at cup-of-tea time at 3.30. I showed you yesterday where that clip-board is, showing those in the dining room or in their rooms at 5.30, and there's a list of those who have gone on the trip on a separate board in the same place.'

Nicky sat and listened and sorted her indoor shoes out while Stella was talking, and she thought all the instructions were over now, because Stella moved over to the large desk and sat down. Then she suddenly turned round to Nicky again. 'Oh, I don't think I told you yesterday, Nicky. There's an understanding among all the staff that if they need to see me for any reason, or if they want just a private chat about something, I'm always available for that in here at two o' clock each day, at the shift change-over time. So this is just to tell you that that is available to you, too. If you want to know anything, or if there's anything on your mind, feel free to ask me.

'Oh, and one other thing, If I ever need to consult everyone, or have an urgent meeting for any reason, that time, two o' clock, is when we meet. It's the one time in the day when everyone is here, either coming or going. That includes Sam. The only person who would not be here would be the nurse on duty the night before, but I can always see her just after six in the morning, when she's finishing and everyone's getting up and preparing for breakfast, or I can just phone her at home. I just ask everyone who has been on the morning shift, six-till-two, to wait behind for a few minutes, and that does it. By the way, our morning shift starts at six, but breakfasts are not available until seven.'

Stella did not return to the desk, but turned and went to the door, just as Linda came bursting through it, ready for the afternoon.

'Oh, hello, Linda. You will already know that Maggie's taken eight of the guests in the bus to Stamford and Rutland water. You haven't met our new carer, Nicky, yet, have you?' Linda beamed with pleasure and the two ladies met with a handshake and an exchange of pleasantries, 'So between the two of you, Linda, if you could deal with both lounges and all the units, the dining room, afternoon tea and the evening snacks, OK? The lists for the trip and the dining room are on the dining room door.'

With that, she continued downstairs, and Linda resumed beaming at Nicky. 'It really is good to meet you, Nicky. As there's just the two of us, we'll go round together, shall we, and get it done twice as quickly?'

'OK by me.'

'Let's start by having a look at that list on the dining room door.' Linda took Nicky's elbow in a most friendly manner, and they both went back out of the office door and quickly down the steps.

'Yes, that's the usual lot that go on the trips,' mused Linda, as she looked rapidly down the list for the trip. 'Maggie's taking two heart problems there, with Martin and Margery, and Marsha and May are asthmatic, although this kind of weather is not likely to bother them, but the other four, Vic, June, Lew and Mick are a happy and healthy bunch of people.

'Let's make a start in the lounges. It seems no-one has put a film on this afternoon, so those in there will be snoozing in front of the usual TV afternoon fare – quizzes, old sit-com series, drama series about hospitals and police – you know.'

Sure enough, that is what they found in the kitchen lounge. In the laundry lounge, there was only one person, Matt, reading his newspaper.

'He won't want to talk because he's quite deaf and often forgets to switch on his hearing aid when he's reading,' Linda whispered to Nicky. Then she went and stood in front of him and tapped on his paper so that he would notice.

'Are you plugged in, Matt?' she asked loudly. 'Turn up your hearing aid, then. Look, while it's almost empty, we're going to vacuum this room. OK? Then we'll dust the polished surfaces. OK?'

Matt slowly lowered his paper right onto his lap, and smiled warmly.

'Thanks, Matt,' said Linda, returning the smile. She put her arm round his shoulders, squeezed him a little and patted his back. He couldn't conceal his pleasure as he glanced upwards. Even as he sat in the armchair, it was clear that Matt was a very tall man. Nicky had noticed him yesterday, and thought he looked a bit stern and aloof. She reflected that he probably had been very strong, mentally and physically, in his time, but now was quiet and a bit withdrawn and on his own because of his very poor hearing. Linda, though, thought Nicky, could make anyone melt a bit and smile.

Linda took her time, slowly and gently, when she was reassuring a person, but she was a veritable dynamo when she had fetched the large vacuum cleaner from the laundry and set off round the laundry lounge. She was younger than Linda, but Nicky worked up a sweat flying round after her with the smaller, battery-operated vac, to do the smaller areas and the nooks and crannies. They had soon dealt with all the surfaces as well. 'You never get rid of dust properly until it's met some moisture,' Linda whispered, brandishing an old, damp dishcloth she had also found in the laundry.

The energy didn't abate much as the two carers went through the rooms along the first corridor. Vic, Jane, Martin and Margery had all gone on the trip. Ella, in No. 5, was usually in her room, but she wasn't now, and then Linda remembered she had seen her in the TV room. Barbara, from No. 6, had also not gone on the trip and had probably taken Ella into the lounge: she always looked out for her, and helped when Ella found anything difficult, which was most of the time.

Lorna, in No. 7, was not in her room, either. 'I don't know where she is, but I know who she'll be with,' Linda told Nicky, with a wink. 'All the staff know that she fancies Chris like mad, and now that there aren't too many people about, they'll be walking around in the grounds, I expect, unless they've gone out into Chignall for a walk. You watch when most people are doing activities all together on Wednesday or Friday afternoons: even across the room, their eyes will be locked on each other. And on Thursdays, when people are doing board games, you'll see their hands aren't on the table most of the time: they're holding hands under the table, or else, if they have to be on the table, Lorna and Chris are playing footsie underneath. It's very sweet, and we all like it. It seems to be all in good humour and nothing really serious. Maybe they'll surprise us one day, but I doubt it. Chris is quite fit and he has been a good footballer in his time, and he doesn't half sing loudly when we have any community singing. Lorna, though, seems much older than Chris, and when she isn't with him, she seems very much on her own. Still, she's certainly got all her marbles, so we'll see.'

Maurice, who lived in No. 8, was not in his room, either. 'H'm. I haven't seen him about,' said Linda, as they tidied round once more and cleaned down his washbasin and collected his towels for the laundry. 'Perhaps he's gone out, too, because you can't miss hearing him, because of his walk. He doesn't so much walk as shuffle – little tiny, shunting steps in his slippers, which he wears all the time. And when he's out, going down the street with his shoes on, he looks all the time as if he's going to totter forward and land on his nose. But he doesn't: his little steps always seem to get him where he's going. I don't like to laugh because it would hurt him, but it really is quite amusing at times.'

They met Lew as he was walking down the corridor, having just left his room. Nicky realised immediately that he was an overpowering personality compared with the other guests. He smiled and laughed a lot, had quite a ruddy complexion, and often made little jokes and quips in his speech. But he was very friendly, and a really good humour came through all his banter. He asked Nicky where she lived, and how big her family was. He seemed most interested in her father and his work, not the occasional jobs for the undertaker, but his main job of selling electric fires. He knew someone who had worked at Anscombe's, and was knowledgeable about different types of electric fire, and which retailer and department store were selling them these days. The hints for Nicky about his love of amateur singing and entertaining as a bit of a comedian, were in his loud voice and lively manner. While they were both talking, Linda had ignored them, gone into Lew's room and tidied round, cleaned and sorted out the en-suite and done some work with the battery hand-vac. By the time Nicky had broken off from his attention, and Lew was continuing his journey down the corridor, Linda was coming out of the room, having finished it.

'OK. That's this corridor done, Nicky. Now let's go and get the teas organised before we do the other one. There's no-one wants tea on this first corridor because they're all out. Can you just check the other corridor, Nicky? I think there may be Sid, Dennis and Christine in their rooms there, though I can't remember who was watching TV. Anyway, if you check all those rooms, I'll ask Matt in the laundry lounge and all the TV-watchers, who wants tea. I'll serve them and then do ours in the office. I don't know if Stella is still in there.'

After her usual energetic whizz-round, Linda had served Matt and the TV-watchers and had taken a tray for the carers and Stella upstairs. Nicky had found Dennis and Christine in their rooms, 15 and 16, and soon got tea to them.'

'All quiet?' asked Stella in the office.

'Yes, pretty much,' answered Linda. 'Lorna and Chris are out somewhere, and we don't know where Maurice is.'

'Not much change there, then.'

'Dennis and Christine are in their rooms,' added Nicky, 'but I don't know where Sid is, and he's not on the trip.'

'Oh, don't worry about where he is.' Linda sounded very confident. 'He'll be around in the gardens somewhere. He loves to spend nearly all day in the gardens. We have to go and fetch him for his lunch sometimes. You'll get used to him, Nicky. He used to work for the 'Parks and Public Gardens' department of the Council in Gainsford, and he thinks he still does. He just loves everything that grows. He talks to the plants, trees and flowers, strokes their leaves, tells them he loves them, and when he smells them you can see him try and give them a kiss. There'll be a bee inside one of those blooms one day, and Sid'll be so close he'll swallow it, and then there'll be such a to-do.' Stella laughed politely, looking at Nicky to see whether she was enjoying this strange description, but Linda continued: 'Tell you what, Nicky, when we've finished the rooms and you've met Dennis and Christine, we'll wander round the gardens for a few minutes and we'll find Sid snooping about somewhere, unless we also come across Chris and Lorna whispering "sweet nothings".'

'The weather's not too bad for walking out,' agreed Stella. 'Make the most of this afternoon, though. I don't know how many of these outings we'll be able to run this Spring and Summer, before we have to start cancelling them.'

Linda looked hard at Stella over the rim of her teacup as she drank. 'Oh, Jo told me,' she said, after a few seconds. 'You're getting quite worried about this virus thing that's supposed to be spreading from China, aren't you?'

The room was quiet. 'Yes, I am,' said Stella, after a short pause. 'Something like that was always potentially going to happen. We've had a few scares in recent years, you know. There was Asian 'flu in the fifties, and more recently, there's been "bird 'flu", SARS, and some people were really worried about Ebola two years ago. I only hope they watch this one carefully, that's all.' Nicky and Linda looked steadily into their teacups while saying nothing and wondering what Stella might mean exactly, and what they could do about it.

After a few minutes, they took theirs and Stella's tea trays to the kitchen and collected all those in the lounges. Before they went for Dennis's and Christine's tea things, they did a "quick whizz round", as Linda called it, in Mick's, Chris's and Matt's rooms. Mick was out, Matt would be still reading his paper, and Chris was still out, somewhere unknown, with Lorna. May was on the trip, Sid was still in the garden, and then they came to Dennis's room.

'Oh, show us what you're making now, Dennis,' Linda called as they entered. 'Oh…isn't that good? What do you call it?'

Dennis spent a lot of time in his room making models. Aeroplanes were perhaps his favourite models to make – not too large, but delicate and they could be displayed on stands leaning at different angles, as he once explained to Linda. 'This one's a Tiger Moth,' Dennis answered, 'one of the earliest planes ever manufactured. It's good for me, because it's a bi-plane, so that's four wings, two on each side, with the delicate wing struts and stays in the middle holding them together. The tail-plane is very delicate, and I'm proud of the little ailerons, the little flaps on the trailing edges of the lower wings.'

'You've even got little men sitting in the seats,' chirped in Nicky.

'Ah well,' said Dennis, looking up and giving Nicky a smile as well as a glance, 'one's the pilot and the one behind navigates and does the jobs that the plane is for. They had just been invented, and were actually used in the first World War, but not for firing at the enemy. It didn't seem to occur to them at first to use a plane as a shooting machine. They used them for reconnaissance, to see where the troops were and exactly what was happening on each battlefield. They also transported a few things and I suppose they would have been very vulnerable if the small arms below shot at them.'

'Well, you live and learn,' Nicky enthused. 'I think it's lovely. What's that thing sticking out underneath at the back?'

'It's called a skid,' replied Dennis. 'It just gives a little stability when it lands. Don't forget this plane would land on grass.' He smiled again as Nicky nodded.

The two carers then collected the tray and left Dennis's room.

'We have another interesting character in number sixteen, next door,' said Linda. Christine is not very talkative, but she loves doing things, and making things. She's very good at crafts, and is very precise about everything. She must have everything exactly in its place, and gets really upset if they're not how she wants them.'

As they went in, Christine was busy with a small piece of material on her table.

'Busy, Christine? You've left your tea, look. Drink it up quickly, before it goes cold.'

There was no suggestion of Linda telling her off, or being critical.

'Ooh!' said Christine. 'Oh, yes.' She gulped it down very quickly. Linda could get these people to do things by speaking very gently, whatever she was saying, Nicky realised. She was really beginning to admire her character. Everything she did and said was all designed to help and guide someone else, including Nicky, as she took her round.

'What have you got here, then, Christine?' asked Nicky. Christine sat looking down at some designs on her table, not volunteering to start the conversation. 'Is it very colourful embroidery?' Nicky continued, 'or would you call it tapestry?' she asked, noticing that there were some large pieces underneath the table, contained in light frames.

'She does lots of these little pieces, Nicky,' Linda continued. 'Often they have people's names embroidered, and she gives them to people, for their birthday or an anniversary of some sort. I think they're very pretty and cleverly done. Some designs are beds of flowers, and Christine sometimes does little pictures, with cottages, or miniature castles, but all are very colourful, like little miniature tapestries.'

'No, no, not tapestry.' Christine suddenly began to speak. 'And they're not just embroidery, either. This is called cross-stitch embroidery, and it's good for lettering or designs or small pictures in the middle of a piece of cloth. Tapestry is for larger designs, and you have to work the colours in with the weft, and have special stitches at each side with the selvage.' Once she was talking on something she knew about, Christine was full of confidence and her eyes shone.

'Well, I think they're absolutely lovely, so colourful and detailed. I bet people are happy to have them as gifts. Hey, Christine,' – and Linda put her face very close to the old lady's – 'will you do one for me, when I retire from here?'

Christine's face straightened. She looked at her in alarm. 'You're not retiring, Linda. You can't leave here!'

'No, no.' Linda put one hand on each shoulder so that she could look at her full in the face. 'No, no, Christine, I'm not retiring. I would never leave you.' Christine visibly relaxed. 'You keep up the good work, though, and we'll call back on you later.' Nicky put one of the designs she had been looking at, down at the side of the table. Christine moved across and snatched it up, darting a vicious look at Nicky, and moved it somewhere else. Linda looked across and smiled at Nicky, who took the point.

The tea things were taken out onto a trolley in the corridor, and there was a "quick whizz round" the rooms of June and Marsha, who were both out on the trip, and Linda and Nicky went on their way to sort out the dining room for the evening. The list told them that everyone was in the dining room for the evening and so they would need cutlery for three tables for four and three tables for two.

It was just after half-past four, but Nicky and Linda could see that the trip was back and guests were making their way to their rooms. It was soup and quiche for supper tonight, and they soon got the soup ready to go, and they set the bread for the toast, and the cups and teapots for the end of the meal.

When everything was set ready for five-thirty, Linda turned, with a very satisfied look, to Nicky. 'OK, then? We'd better just look for our waifs and strays before we're ready to serve this lot. By the way, I've seen Maurice, that we didn't know about earlier. He was just walking along the corridor with two or three who had been out, though I'm sure he wasn't on the trip. He's probably been out for a walk in Chignall this afternoon. And Chris and Lorna will come sneaking in from somewhere, no doubt. So that just leaves one – Sid,' said Linda. 'Let's go round the garden and find him,' she said, with a mischievous smile at Nicky.

It was mild for the time of year, and Linda enjoyed venturing into the garden, going beyond the closely-mown lawn, and circling round to the furthest boundary, where the land had been left rather rough and uncultivated with a wild, untamed look. They were through the winter now, and February had been mild and very wet, with floods over much of Shropshire, and the largest parts of Herefordshire, Gloucestershire and Worcestershire. There was serious flooding with whole farms under water, grazing livestock drowned, and those who lived in farmhouses having to row in boats to the nearest landfall. But there lingered at the outer, uncultivated boundary of the Woodside Lodge gardens, the bravest little flowers of winter – among the rocky little hillocks and tree roots, patches of snowdrops, as if there had been a snowstorm and they had fallen from the sky.

And there they saw Sid. There was a bench nearby where he had left his bag, but when they saw him he was kneeling down in a patch of snowdrops, which were well past their best, and he was cradling a lone bloom in his hand and looking at it. He smiled as they approached him – a wide, innocent smile that showed his happiness at seeing them.

'He's a lovely man, though not too clever,' said Linda, in an undertone. 'He's supposed to have had learning difficulties, but he loves flowers, parks and gardens, and I think there's nothing that he doesn't know about what grows in them. He's genuinely happy to see us.' Then, raising her voice, she asked, 'What have you got there, then, Sid? What have you got to show us?'

'Oh, one of my favourite flowers. They belong to February really, but this clump is still carrying on.' He looked down at the bloom in his hand. 'They grow in the hard days, the bleak times when nothing else will break through the earth, but they point towards Spring and tell us of warmer days to come. They're not afraid of the frost, and they bring us joy, before the sturdy daffodils, the feminine charms of the crocuses, and then the glamour of the tulips. But they're the first, and the bravest. Yet they are so simple and humble. There's nothing fancy about them, no showing off beautiful petals or stems. They're just small and pure. I think they're my favourites and I love them.'

'You should put your thoughts about your flowers into poetry some day,' said Linda, reaching out to him with feeling.

'Never was no good at writin',' he said, getting off his knees. 'Just give me the flowers.' Then he pointed back to the building. 'Daffs comin' up already there, look,' he said, 'and down the end of that path you might just see a crocus.'

'Come on, Sid,' said Linda, putting her arm around him. 'We love you like you love your flowers, and I think we'd better be getting back for something to eat.'

He picked up his bag from the seat, so happy to have the attention of the two ladies, and all three walked happily back to the Lodge.

Back at the dining room, the soup, quiche, and tea were soon served and consumed, with just four of the guests wanting toast as well.

'Thanks for letting me come round with you, today, Linda,' said Nicky, looking warmly into her face.

Linda gripped her forearm, with feeling. 'Pleasure. You're one of us now,' she said.

Nicky made sure that she did the major share of the washing up and sorting out of the kitchen, and walked around both lounges to see who was about, but most of the guests had gone back to their rooms.

Finally, she went back up to the office to change into her outside clothes. Stella was there, at the large desk.

'OK, Nicky?'

'Oh, yes, thanks. What have we got tomorrow afternoon?'

'H'm. You'll see,' said Stella with a smile. 'Goodnight.'

'Goodnight.'

Chapter 3

No, no. Don't go down and put the TV on in the kitchen lounge, Nicky,' said Linda quickly. Linda and Nicky were sharing the afternoon shift again, and Nicky had suggested that she should go downstairs, make sure the dining room was cleared after lunch, and then set the afternoon going by settling the TV-watchers.

'You see,' Linda explained, 'when we ask individual guests to do certain things, because we know it's necessary or because it's good for them, we use gentle persuasion and good humour.' She smiled broadly as if to reinforce the point. 'We suggest and cajole and smile a lot. It always works. They say they understand and set about it. But there are times when we're trying to organise them all together, and we have to arrange things so that they don't have much option.

'That applies to Wednesday afternoons. Half of them have been out on a trip on Tuesday, so the week livens up and gets more active. Then on Wednesdays, we don't start the TV going because we want as many as possible to go into the laundry lounge.

'It's called "Music and Movement", and a young physio, Julia Nash, comes to get them moving. That's right, isn't it, Kath?' Linda appealed to the nurse, Kath Taylor, that Nicky had met in the office about five minutes ago. She had just finished the morning six-to-two shift, and was having a brief sit-down before going home. She was quick to reinforce what Linda was saying.

'Yes. It's really important that as many as possible take part in "Music and Movement". Whatever they've done on Tuesday, we must make sure they move as much as possible, especially arms and back muscles. Keep the circulation going and the joints as supple as is realistic. It really is the worst thing for them to spend long periods sitting or slumped down in the armchairs in front of the TV. That's why we encourage them to be in their rooms or going about the building or the grounds or into the village in the mornings. And we don't want too many afternoons just dozing in front of the TV. So it's not switched on until Julia is ready in the laundry lounge. After lunch on Wednesday, she's got a way of getting them out of their chairs and into the laundry lounge, though most have to sit down once they get there. And how does she get them in there? Simple. Music loud enough to be heard around the building. And what sort of music? Well, the tunes and the groups and the pop songs they all remember from their youth.'

'When would that have been, then?' Nicky was trying to guess.

'The sixties,' replied Kath. 'Anyone in their seventies now, and that's most of them, was a teenager in the sixties, and they'll remember all the pop stars and the groups. More than anything, they'll remember the beat, because it was at the end of the fifties and beginning of the sixties that rock'n'roll started. You know, Elvis Presley and the Beach Boys in the States, Cliff Richard in this country, and then the Beatles.'

Nicky and Linda had heard of these, but were not really impressed.

'What was it about that music, then, that made it so well-known, and so many of those stars famous?' asked Linda.

'Well, it wasn't my era,' said Kath. 'I wasn't a teenager until the turn of the century, but I think it's not so much the music as the nostalgia. When our guests hear a Beach Boys song, it sends them back to when they were young, the people they knew, the places they went to, and they get all their old feelings back. That's why they love the music so much: it stimulates that part of the brain where all those memories reside.' Kath began to get more excited. 'Psychiatrists use nostalgia. If they get their patients to recall where they lived after the war, or when their team won the FA Cup, or the years they spent working in Nottingham, it seems to get their minds flowing more freely. They remember all sorts of details, and it makes them happy. You notice how many of our guests love to watch old films on the TV. They prefer them to modern programmes. It takes them back to what they knew, how they expect people to behave, and what they talked about then.'

As if on cue, Julia, downstairs in the laundry lounge, got the music started with the Beach Boys belting out a song called "The Sloop John B".

'Now, you'll see if you go downstairs now, all those who have been sitting in the armchairs in the kitchen lounge, will be waking up, getting up with more enthusiasm than usual, and going through to get a place in the other room. They can't help themselves. They just go, and they'll all be looking so happy, calling out little jokes and comments. They'll be unable to sit still and stop their feet tapping when they sit down. Ha! We've got a lot to thank Elvis for.' Kath laughed, leaned back, collected her bags that she had brought for the morning's work, and got up to go home.

Linda and Nicky went down the stairs. Linda said she would go and tidy up the kitchen lounge and dining room, and then she would see Nicky in the laundry lounge later. Sure enough, when Nicky arrived there, it was quite full. Everyone was looking happy, and nearly all of them were tapping their feet, or lightly slapping the chair-arm. Now it was the Walker brothers, singing that the sun was not going to shine any more, and when it finished and the tapping ceased, Julia explained that she wanted to get arms moving for the next record, and she demonstrated a vertical and then horizontal stretching of the arms. A tune on brass instruments by someone called Herb Alpert followed, and Julia said it was called "Spanish Flea", and would everyone imagine that they felt fleas tickling them as they sat there and they had to keep snatching at them and swiping them to the beat of the music. Much exaggeration of this went on, accompanied by considerable laughter. Later, the more supple guests were swinging arms, bending down, turning round and working themselves up a little.

So the early afternoon went on, and when the Supremes announced that "You can't hurry love", all those who could were invited to stand and then they did a "knees up" to the beat in what looked like a stiff-legged running on the spot. Those who did not want to stand, just clapped.

Linda returned, and smiled at Nicky obviously enjoying it all and joining in with all the actions, encouraging some of the slower people.

'You see, there are fourteen people sitting round in this room,' said Linda, and in the next pause, she asked how many wanted tea at the end of the "Music and Movement", which would be just before three o'clock.

'We'll go and switch it on and serve it out at three,' she told Nicky. 'That's what we usually do, and it makes a break before we do another lively session later. You'll see.'

The music slowed down a bit later, but everybody was really in the mood, and when Chris Montez sang "The more I see you", three or four people stood up and jogged around a little. Lorna and Chris moved quite well in a loose embrace, and in their own way they added to the feeling around the room.

Linda told Nicky that Ella would have been too nervous to come to the music, and so she would go to her room later, and suggest that she would take her for a walk round the garden. She suggested that Nicky did the same for Maurice, who was physically very awkward when it came to co-ordinated movement of any kind, and Nicky would have to be very careful that he didn't fall. If he didn't want to, Linda's next suggestion was that she had noticed that Matt was not in the room, possibly because he couldn't hear the music very well, but he was usually amenable to walking and might feel flattered if Nicky called on him to ask.

'Remember he has a bit of a weak heart, though,' Linda said more seriously, 'and don't overdo it.'

After the two carers had served afternoon tea a little early, and after she had done the bulk of the washing-up, Nicky went back towards the laundry lounge to be greeted with loud, noisy laughter. In fact, Margery, who was one of the more recently-arrived guests at Woodside Lodge, and who was sitting near the door, was shrieking, beside herself with mirth. This emphasised her size, because she was a rather large lady and was trying to roll about in her chair. Linda joined Nicky to watch this, before they went off for their walks. There was still the same number of guests in the room and they were all looking at Lew, who was in the centre of the carpet, on the floor, with all the chairs pulled into a circle round him.

He was pretending to be a chicken, and so was Mick, and they must have been doing some sort of drama together, Nicky thought. What was so funny was the way Lew was squatting right down on his ankles and then strutting about clucking and tipping forward to peck unseen titbits of food from the ground. Lew and Mick must have been the only guests who could squat down like that, let alone strut about and cluck. Mick was doing the same, and overbalanced and lay on his side, so that necessitated another raucous burst of squawking while he got upright again. By this time, Lew had gone a bit quiet and sat still on one or two occasions. He popped his eyes wide and went red in the face with straining. After a few seconds of that, he collapsed forward onto the floor and strutted slowly away, leaving a shiny white china egg on the floor behind him.

'Where did that come from?' Vic asked June, as they sat next to each other near Nicky.

'Out of his bum,' said June. 'Where do you think? He's just laid it.' Mick did the same with another egg, and then the two of them had a confrontational squawking match.

The two of them went out and came back as people to watch Marsha, who was always willing to do anything, parade down the side of the room, and give a really sexy wiggle as she walked. The little drama ended with Lew pretending to be a TV interviewer asking Marsha about an exciting play that she had been watching. To do that, Lew walked over and stole Julia's microphone as a prop. Julia usually stayed to watch this second half of the afternoon.

Linda and Nicky went down the corridors to look for Ella, Maurice and Matt, while the rest of the fun went on. 'In the second half of the afternoon, they play "house-party-type games," explained Linda. 'That is charades, but not the modern version which has been on TV, with codes for films, books, the number of words, and so on. This is the older version of the game where you have a word and enact each syllable and then put it together to guess the word. They can also do it with the names of towns or places, or a famous person's name, or old song titles. It's great fun, because they've already been warmed up with the "Music and Movement". They divide into two teams, so that one team enacts while the other guesses and then vice-versa. There are other party games as well. There's one called "Nuts in May". I've seen that one with the chicken that Lew was doing before. Everyone has, and they know the word, "exciting", but it's so funny they keep asking him to do it again and again.'

They had reached Ella's door, and so Linda went in to talk and entice her out, while Nicky went to fetch out the men, if they were willing. They were, and all the walkers met a few minutes later in the extensive garden. They met Sid, of course, still rhapsodising about the remaining snowdrops. He said he had more news, though, and that was that there were four or five crocuses in a cultivated border at the back of the corridor where he lived in No. 14. He said he could see them out of his back window. 'It's Spring,' he said, dancing a little jig. Then he announced that to the side of the snowdrop bed, there were daffodil shoots pushing up a bit higher than they were, though there were no blooms yet. Maurice also proclaimed that it was Spring again and shuffled around to do another jig. Unfortunately, that set Sid off adjusting his clothes. He kept twisting his arm inside his jacket sleeve, and he did this over and over again, as if it irritated him. In between twists, he hitched his trousers up, so that became a part of his clothes routine as well. Poor Sid. He had so many obsessive habits that usually amused people, but sometimes annoyed them.

They all returned to the Lodge, pleased by the news that it was salmon mousse for supper, as well as the usual soup and toast. Linda and Nicky went straight to the dining room as soon as they returned, to set the cutlery and place mats. The guests must have all been made very sociable by the music and games in the afternoon, because they had all signed up for the dining room – everyone, that is, except Barbara, who wanted to be served in her room. Linda went to see to her, because she couldn't have the salmon, being allergic to fish of all kinds, but she happily settled for some of the quiche left over from Tuesday night and un-chilled.

The meal went smoothly and happily and when Nicky had washed up with Linda, and had done all the cleaning and putting away, she stayed in the kitchen lounge for a while with the TV-watchers. There were only four of them.

As she went upstairs to fetch her bag to go home, Jo arrived and greeted her warmly. Nicky thought again how this lovely lady exuded confidence and authority. She admired those qualities.

Nicky did notice, however, that as they both reached the top of the stairs and went into the office, Stella was already there, at the desk, as she had been on the other evenings. Jo had come to take over the nine-to-six shift. Stella briefly greeted Nicky, but seemed unusually pleased to see Jo. When Jo noticed the steady, unwavering and silent look Stella gave her, she returned the look.

As she picked up her bag, Nicky glanced round at these two strong, competent women. She sensed a tension in the air, and quickly realised that she would be welcome to stay not one moment longer, and scurried down the stairs and walked briskly home.

'Linda's not here today,' Stella greeted Nicky as she arrived at the office the next day. 'She's off Thursday and Friday, and she'll be back for the weekend on the early shift, six-till-two. We rotate people through the shifts so that they don't get fed up with the same routines and the same tasks. Only, I wanted you to stay on afternoons all through your first week so that you would get to know the afternoon activities for a week. Here's Laura, and she'll work with you today and tomorrow. Much the same routine, but different activities.'

Laura stood beaming at Nicky. If ever there was a warm welcome, this was it, she thought. Above the smiling eyes, Nicky looked down onto a mass of curls, for Laura was shorter than the younger girl. There was very little expanse of forehead to be seen, for the curls spilled over the front of her head down to her eyes. The face was broad, the nose and mouth were of normal proportions, and the whole happy face was suffused by the smile.

'Welcome to Woodside,' said Laura, 'home to Stella and eighteen guests, and home to us while we work here,' she said happily. 'I understand you saw Lew doing his party piece as a chicken yesterday.'

Nicky rolled her eyes to the ceiling and then looked down onto the curls again. 'Yes.' She laughed at the memory. 'It was one of the funniest things I've ever seen. I think it's a better way of playing charades than I've seen them do on TV.'

'Well, I suppose that's how it was played in the days before there were so many films and so many actors and actresses. The Victorians had to entertain themselves at house-parties. Anyway, Nicky,' – Laura changed the subject – 'let's get downstairs, see that the lunch is all cleared away and the dining room is a bit ship-shape, and then we can get the board games out. It's board games on Thursday afternoons, not quite as popular as jigsaws, but good enough and a little noisy sometimes.'

There was nothing more to be said, just a quick nod towards Stella and Kath, who was gathering her bags to go home, and the two girls, friends already by all appearances, went down to get the afternoon moving.

Lunch had been over for some time, but the smell of custard and apple pie still lingered as Nicky straightened the furniture in the dining room. It was always a comforting smell, Nicky thought, and always reminded her of Sunday lunches at home throughout her childhood.

The board games were brought out of a spacious sideboard cupboard in the laundry lounge, and the card tables had already been set round by the players in twos and fours. Draughts, snakes and ladders, ludo, dominoes, scrabble and chess – they were all there, and four hardy souls were settling down to what was probably a marathon game of monopoly. After the initial shunting around, everything looked as if it was set to last well beyond tea-break time.

'We'll get round the rooms, and see if everything's OK, or if anyone wants anything,' said Laura. 'You'll see that today, because it's quiet, a few visitors come around, but the guests usually take them off to their rooms rather than sit around in the games room. There's a bit of a build-up of visitors towards the weekend.'

With that, Laura, just as Linda had done, assumed that Nicky would like it if they went around together. They looked into the kitchen lounge, but there were only two people watching live TV in there. 'That's about normal,' muttered Laura. 'There must have been a dozen people starting those board games, so that only leaves six others. Two are in here, and four in their rooms. That's about right.

'I noticed it was Margery and Jane in there,' continued Laura, 'and you do need to watch Margery when she's moving from sitting down to going back to her room. Apparently, she is liable to fall every so often. She's not been here long, but she has already fallen once, and, what with her size, it was quite an elaborate performance getting her going again.'

'Oh, Linda warned me about someone like that yesterday,' said Nicky, touching her hair and trying to remember who it was.

'Maurice, I should think,' volunteered Laura.

'Yes.'

'Yes. I call him "shuffler" because of how he goes along. He's a very nice chap, though. He's thoughtful and a bit quiet, but he's got a good sense of humour when you get talking to him.'

The first room they came to was Vic's at No.1. He was out, so they went in, tidied up a bit with the hand-vac and then cleaned his washbasin and toilet in the en-suite. They knew Jane's and Margery's rooms would be empty, so Laura took No.2, Jane's, and Nicky, Margery's. They were both very tidy, with the beds made, and the en-suites didn't really want washing down, but they did it all the same. Ella was sitting quietly, apparently studying the TV, but not having switched it on.

'Wipe your nose, dear,' said Laura, pleasantly. 'Would you like the TV switched on, so you can watch it?' Ella was going to nod in agreement after she had wiped her nose, but before she could, Barbara came bustling in.

'Oh, don't switch it on,' she called out to Laura. 'I asked her at lunch if she wanted to walk out this afternoon, but she will have forgotten. Come on, Ella dear, let's go and get some fresh air.'

Ella was quite compliant, and stood up while Barbara got her coat, stood behind her and held out the arms for her to put it on. Barbara continued to ignore Laura while Ella got herself comfortable, but then gave Laura a quick nod and she encouraged Ella to go through the door as she held it open for her.

'Will you have her back for afternoon tea?' Laura asked quietly. Another nod, and they were going down the corridor, while Laura made the bed and washed down the en-suite.

'That's the first six rooms empty, then,' Laura said, as she checked where Nicky was. 'Lorna is No.7. She'll be playing games in the lounge with Chris. At least, their hands will be on the board, but they'll be playing footsie under the table all afternoon.'

Maurice, Lew and Mick were all out, probably in the games room, and they found Matt deeply absorbed in watching a film on TV. He had the volume turned right up, and seemed to resent Laura being in there with him, but she did not want to come back later, and so went round with the battery hand-vac quickly and took a peremptory look in the en-suite.

Nicky, therefore, went into May's room on her own and found that May had a visitor.

'Ah! Just the lady I would like to see,' said a fairly tall, pleasant-looking man as he rose from his chair to greet Nicky. Without letting May say anything, he continued: 'May said the carer might be round soon. Let me introduce myself. I'm Jack, May's nephew. She's a widow, as you know, and she has no children, so I'm her nearest relative. Once the Council has made its small contribution, I pay the rest of her fees here.

'There's something I've had on my mind lately, about May, and she's just told me she agrees with me. Being in here has done her a lot of good, because she's much more lively and energetic than she used to be, and she tells me she doesn't feel tired all the time like she used to.'

'Yes. I'm really happy,' added May, 'and June and I, we get on really well.'

'What I was wondering was whether she could come off those thyroxine tablets she takes every day. There hardly seems to be any reason for her to stay in here now. It was because she was so depressed and lacking any kind of energy that I applied for her to come.'

'Oh, I don't want to leave.' May seemed a little alarmed. 'I'm so happy,' she repeated.

Nicky had the feeling that she should not discuss this kind of thing with a guest or with any visitor. She over-reacted, went over and pressed the button on the bedside cabinet that activated a pager. 'I'm afraid I can't discuss this kind of thing with you,' she said, apologetically. 'I'm only here to look after people and to clean and to help the guests with anything physical that they can't manage.' Jack seemed disappointed, flapped his hands slightly with a little frustration and sat down again. 'I've sent for the manager, Stella Holden, and she'll be here in a minute.'

Neither of the nurses were at the Lodge during the afternoon after two o' clock, but there was always one of them on call. However, at the moment, Stella was on the premises, and it seemed like no time at all before she came through the door very briskly, carrying a small bag, which she immediately threw on the bed.

'What is it?'

'Oh, it's Jack, May's nephew who looks after her affairs,' began Nicky. 'He was wondering about May's medication, and started to ask me about it, so I sent for you.'

The alertness dissolved from Stella's face and shoulders and she visibly relaxed, but at the same time, shook her head and glared at Nicky. 'No, Nicky,' she said. 'You press that button only in an emergency,' and she emphasised the "only" with a vigorous shaking up and down of her forearm. 'I could see it was number thirteen ringing, and I know May is normally quite strong, and so any sudden alarm like that usually means that a fit person is choking.'

Laura had left Matt's room and had come into May's room when she saw Stella had arrived and had gone in, and now all three ladies and Jack were silent in the presence of Stella's authority. She turned to Jack and her face softened. 'Mr Scott, you are quite at liberty to discuss May's medication, but not with one of the carers; with me in the office or, if I am not here, with one of the nurses.'

'I'm sorry if I stepped out of line, Miss Holden.' Jack Scott rose from his chair again. 'I just wanted to let everyone know how pleased I am that May seems so happy here, after how run-down and depressed she was before she came. I wondered if she could come off those tablets she's been taking since she came in.'

There was another shaking of the head. 'No, Mr Scott. May has one levothyroxine tablet per day to replace the thyroxine hormone in which she had been diagnosed as being deficient by Dr Attwood. The brand name is Levoxyl. It could be that May is so much better because of the prescribed tablets, which our nurses make sure she takes. Whichever it is, any change in her medication can occur not because of what you or I say, but on the advice of Dr Attwood at the Gainsford surgery. You have your opinion, Mr Scott, but what you will have to do is ask the surgery for a telephone appointment with Dr Attwood, and then tell him what you have told us. He may re-examine her, possibly with a blood test, but all that is entirely up to him.'

'Oh, yes. I'm sorry,' said Jack. 'I was just visiting and thought I would ask, but I'll do as you suggest, and I do apologise that you have been brought here when it was not necessary.'

'Alright, Mr Scott. No harm done.' Stella was back to her good humour now, and smiled towards May and Jack. She retrieved her small bag, and in a relaxed, friendly tone, she said to Nicky: 'Would you fetch May and Jack a cup of tea if they want one, and then it's about time that you and Laura went round everyone offering tea. When you've done that, Nicky, would you come and have your tea in the office with me, and you might as well come as well, Laura. Good afternoon, Mr Scott.'

When Laura and Nicky had taken tea and cake to those who asked for it in the kitchen lounge and in the laundry lounge as they pored over their board games, and also to May and her nephew, and Matt and Christine who were busy in their rooms, they went upstairs to see Stella, as she had asked. They hadn't found Sid, but they knew he would be in the grounds somewhere, and assumed he did not want tea.

'Oh, hello,' Stella greeted them warmly. 'Sit down and let's have tea now. It's OK, Nicky. I'm sure you will have learnt your lesson now about paging me or Jo or Kath. We'll nearly always be in the office here, if and when it goes off, especially at night. We go downstairs from this point and through a couple of doors and we're at the units, so I always like to boast that we could be at the appropriate room in no more than two minutes.'

They sorted everything out and began sipping their tea. 'When you started on Monday, Nicky, I told you there was a list of all the guests who were on medication, and you can consult it if you ever notice anything that worries you. It is in the desk drawer, here. But only Jo and Kath can use it, apart from me, in the sense of getting anything out of those locked casements up there against the wall, and administering it to a guest. Whoever is on duty in the morning makes sure that medication has been taken and recorded, and the same when they or I take over on the night shift. There is plenty of time in the morning, because we start at six, but breakfast for guests is not until seven. Anyway, Nicky, if you could just look at your copy, and Laura, this will be a reminder to you, too, and I'll run down who needs what. There are two versions, one classified by guest, and one categorised by medication and who has it.'

Stella moved a few papers round, changed her glasses, and began. 'You would expect a number of heart problems with elderly people, and we have four, Margery, Martin, Mick and Matt. Those four all take warfarin. That is a blood-thinner, Nicky. It prevents blood clots forming. Levels of warfarin in the blood are tested regularly by the GP or hospital, but you need to notice blood in the urine, black stools or bruising, which could mean too much thinning of the blood. Martin and Mick have beta-blockers, because they have high blood pressure. We have to reduce the blood pressure, but beta-blockers have side-effects, and I don't think a doctor would prescribe them for Margery. The commonest tablet is Amlodipine, and Matt and Margery have that each day.

'Type 2 diabetes is also common among our senior citizens these days, and all our four, Lorna, Lew, Dennis and June, take the commonest tablet treatment for that, one metformin once a day. We have to encourage them to exercise if we can. Lorna, Lew and June are OK, but not Dennis. He needs much more encouragement. We also have to be careful of their diet as well, keeping them off sugary or starchy foods. They know that, and should tell you when you serve them at meal-times, but the responsibility is on us to know and to bear it in mind. Unfortunately, we have three guests with arthritis, and that can be very painful. The patients really have to manage it themselves, and they are all referred to their consultant at Brookfields hospital regularly. Different forms of painkillers can be bought and administered without prescription – I am talking about paracetamol, Ibuprofen and codeine – but I want that to be decided and done only by me or Jo or Kath. We could give them an anti-inflammatory, like Naproxin, though never with Ibuprofen. You can't be too careful, and they are under lock and key here. If anyone asks you for any, just say you will have to ask me, Jo or Kath. If anyone has been prescribed morphine for extreme pain, only Jo, Kath or I can inject it. If anyone is generally not too well, we do try to take blood pressure readings as often as possible, especially if they say they feel dizzy, but leave that, again, to me, Jo or Kath. Dizziness can mean low blood pressure, which is dangerous, but it can also mean vertigo, which is also common with elderly guests, though I don't know that we have any at present. Now, we have three people who suffer from asthma. That seems to occur more commonly these days, almost regardless of general health condition. It mostly seems to be caused by an allergic reaction of some kind, and often goes along with hay fever. You can have anti-inflammatory tablets for hay fever, and we have them for general use if they're needed. Anyway, Jane, Marsha and Chris have asthma attacks fairly regularly.

'There are two ways of treating asthma, to prevent it, and to relieve it. The tablets to prevent it are Accolate or Theophylline, taken daily but only if prescribed by a doctor, and we keep the store of them and the nurses administer them. There is also a preventative inhaler, Flutiform, which might make the inhaler's voice sound funny. Relieving asthma, though, is done by an inhaler, and a spacer can be used to make them more effective. Now these are kept in their rooms, in the bedside cabinets. If they are in distress, they need some help immediately, and they operate them, so they have them ready. They can't overdose on them. They contain Salbutamol and the brand name is Ventolin. If they say they've run out, or they're no good, we help them get another one prescribed – the nurses do, that is. So there you have it. Asthma is just one of those things that always seems to be around, though only Jane, Marsha and Chris have it regularly here, as far as I know.

'Please remember that these things I have mentioned are just the common, run-of-the-mill ailments that beset many elderly people the same age as our guests. More advanced nursing care may be referred to the GP surgery or Brookfields hospital. You carers, though, only report things to the nurses, and you have no responsibility after that. Remember also that we are not a nursing home. None of our guests come in here with serious illness, and none of them are bedridden. We are a care home, with nursing. But I insist that we inform the public that we have three NMC registered nurses on our staff, and our guests are safe.

Stella finished her cup of tea quickly, turned round to the desk, and seemed to be looking to Nicky and Laura to get back to work, but suddenly resumed:

'Oh, perhaps there's another thing I should mention, and that is what to do in the case of injury. Many elderly people, including many in care homes, hurt themselves by falling, and often cannot get up. Obviously, you send for me, Jo or Kath if one of us is here, but the first thing to do is to ask about any pain, and try to establish if anything is broken. If that is so, don't move them whatever you do. We'll ring for an ambulance. Moving someone with a broken limb is a skilled business and the paramedics will know what to do. Otherwise, you just try to help to get them to a chair as soon as you can in the circumstances. But an ambulance and paramedics have to come if you tell them someone has fallen.

'I tell you what,' she added, 'we do have people who can't get up out of a chair on occasions. Here's how to deal with that. You stand squarely in front of them , whatever they're sitting in or on and tell them they have to help you get them up, because you can't just lift an inert weight. Then explain that you are linking your right forearm with their right forearm, each holding the other's elbow in the cup of their hand. Demonstrate that calmly before you do anything. Come on, you do that with me, Nicky, as you are sitting there. Then go back to the start, link forearms, and say that on the count of three, you will pull, but they will have to pull on you, too. So then, if that is done, they should come springing up. No bother.' Nicky sprang into Stella's arms. It finished with smiles all round.

'OK, ladies. I'll let you collect up the tea things and finish your rounds. It's cold pork pie portions with salad, I think, for supper, so there are no worries about allergies there. Oh – one more thing – sorry to keep adding them on! Andy Dodds is coming with his keyboard to provide the Friday afternoon entertainment tomorrow. He's good.

'But there are some worrying things on my mind, and I will call staff together at two o' clock tomorrow. In your two cases, you'll have to finish clearing lunch and see that Andy has all he wants and starts getting them singing. Then, I'm afraid it will mean being up here in the office all together. So enjoy the rest of the day, and I'll see you then.'

Chapter 4

Nicky thought it best to arrive a little early on Friday afternoon, as Stella had mentioned meeting all the staff at two o' clock. Stella seemed to be waiting for her as she arrived at a quarter to two.

'A slight change of plan from what I had suggested yesterday, Nicky,' she said. 'Linda can't come in at two, but she can be here at three thirty, so what I've decided is that you and Laura will have to manage your afternoon shift with each of you on your own for a while. I'll see Laura with the others at two, but you need to clear the lunch and set Andy Dodds going on your own and then come up here from tea-break onwards at three-thirty. Don't worry about Andy Dodds, though. He brings his own keyboard, microphone and sound system and he just needs it all plugging in. He knows where to do that, but you hang around and watch him until the guests go into the laundry lounge and he is away. Sam likes to come in and help him to sort out his equipment, so I've asked him to do that, too. Then he can come up here to join the two o' clock meeting. After clearing the lunch, you'll just have to keep an eye on Andy, and I'll have in here Laura, Sam, Maggie and Kath, as they finish their morning stints. Jo is on nights, so I'll have a good chat with her as she starts at nine tonight. Then, would you come here at the end of tea-break, Nicky? I'll see you and Linda then for a while.'

'OK, then, Stella. I'll see you later,' Nicky replied.

Lunch must have been over early, because when Nicky went into the dining room, all the tables had been wiped down and the chairs were neatly re-arranged in their twos and fours. She went into the kitchen to finish things off with washing and cleaning and re-packing the dishes and cutlery. Laura had done this yesterday, Thursday, and told Nicky that the sooner all that was done, Sam was really glad because then he could go home. He lived on his own in a flat in Gainsford, Laura had told her, and he was quite "dishy". She was married, and so was not interested, but it might be a chance for Nicky if she had no boyfriend. She winked as she told her. Well, today I'll get to meet him, thought Nicky, as she pushed into the kitchen through the swing door that returned to its position once you had gone through. She had a surprise. There he was, taller and slimmer than she expected and quite fair. His hair was not straw-coloured, as was the hair of most fair men, but a soft, pale grey colour and so very wispy that it was difficult to say precisely what colour it was. But what she was sure of was that he was fair. He had rather large ears, she thought, and she noticed a row of very white, even and attractive teeth as he smiled. As he said "Hello" in a fairly high-pitched voice,

Nicky noticed at the same time a thick growth of whiskers along the jaw, round the chin, and the width of his top lip. Nicky didn't like to see young men like that, because she thought it made them look a bit dirty and as if they hadn't bothered to shave for a few days, but that was obviously how he liked it, and it was supposed to be very fashionable. She liked the width of his face, the straight nose and his warm eyes as he smiled at her. She returned the smile as warmly as she could manage in her working surroundings.

'We'll soon get this done,' he assured her, 'and I've just seen Andy Dodds's car arriving, so I'll nip into the lounge in a minute or two to help him set up.' He was in such a hurry with the dishes after that, there was no time for any further conversation, and Nicky thought the best way to impress him would be to work fast. He was soon gone, leaving her to finish off and to look at the list for supper before she also headed for the laundry lounge. By the time she arrived, a good number of guests had found seats, and Nicky noticed one or two visitors with them. Nobody had stayed to watch TV in the kitchen lounge. This man was certainly popular for a bit of entertainment at the end of the week.

There did, though, seem to be a bit of a problem. The keyboard was in place and Andy had tested it, but the microphone didn't seem to work and Sam was prodding open a plastic bar carrying several plugs that had leads coming in from the microphone and then going out to the speaker. Sam seemed full of concern and tension as he examined the bar which obviously had a function to do with amplification.

'Nicky, could you please nip upstairs for me and ask Stella if I can come to the three-thirty meeting? I've got a problem here and I must help Andy to get started.' Nicky soon sprinted upstairs, and the answer was, 'Of course.' When she returned, Sam was muttering about an emitter and a collector on a base connected to terminals. He seemed to know more about a connection that did not work than did Andy, who was watching. The frustration and grunting continued for two more minutes. Suddenly, there was slight click under Sam's finger, followed by 'That's it!' from Sam.

Andy started into life, and used his strong voice to quell the restless hubbub that was growing among the guests. He put sudden, sharp, loud energy into "Hello, hello, who's your lady friend?" and by the end of two verses they were all together.

'Could you give out the word sheets so that we can all make a lot more noise, Sam?' asked Andy. Sam skipped along a row of chairs shelling out sheets to the sitters, and gave Nicky a few for her to supply the opposite side. "I'm

Henery the Eighth I am, I am," followed, with a rousing shout or two, and then, slowing a little, Andy made them laugh as they sang "Daddy wouldn't buy me a bow-bow". He invented electronic whines on his guitar and made pitiful faces at the appropriate points. There followed two more rousing numbers with "Boiled beef and carrots" and "Roll out the barrel."

As they were recovering from those noisy songs with laughter and shuffling around in seats, Andy transformed his appearance by instantly fitting on a false white shirt front and a black dicky-bow tie held in place with elastic. In a cultured, sophisticated tone of voice, he then announced he was Cyril Fletcher and was about to recite some odd odes, so would they pin back their "lug-'oles" and listen.

'I'll help out by holding the fort here if you want to nip along to look in the rooms of the first corridor,' Sam whispered to Nicky. 'I'm not at work now, but I'll stay around for a bit. This chap's so talented, I like to study his technique.' Nicky went off to see to things.

A few people looked around at each other with a smirk because when Andy had got into his role and announced, "This is the Tale of Sonia Snell", they knew what to expect. There followed a simple poem in rhyming couplets about a young lady who sat on a painted toilet seat which stuck to her. A number of mini-adventures followed, with a variety of people trying to help with her dilemma. The soft chuckling among the guests rose until it became a cackle of merriment and finally, when he described an operation to remove the seat with a surgeon giving a commentary to watching medical students, it resulted in a burst of guffaws.

Andy had a repertoire of those, but was too experienced to overdo it. He kept the atmosphere going by getting them to sing again. He was not rushing through the afternoon. There was plenty of space in between items for him to change out of his simple costumes and for the guests to chat with each other. When he was at his keyboard, the word sheets had been found and the amplified microphone was working, though kept reasonably low. Andy moved on from music-hall to mid-century songs, some relating to the war, and within the guests' lifetimes.

The war songs were getting into full swing as Nicky returned and stood watching with Sam. She had heard "There'll be bluebirds over the white cliffs of Dover" as she came back along the corridor, and after "Faraway places with strange-sounding names", "We'll meet again" and "I'm forever blowing bubbles", there was a fairly lengthy pause.

'I think we've got two different sorts of monologues coming now,' whispered Sam, and Nicky sat down. Nearly all the guests were in here this afternoon. Even Dennis, Maurice and Christine had come, unusually, and Nicky had decided that she was watching over them best if she just took in the entertainment and watched for any who needed the toilet. She asked Sam to let her know when he thought it was near enough to the end for her to go and set the tea going.

Without needing any kind of costume, though he had a peaked hat and a boy's school cap on the table beside him, Andy put on his Lancashire working-class accent and delivered in fairly quick succession a few short monologue/dramatisations by a comedian called Al Read, who was remembered by a number of the guests. Andy had at one time delivered monologues by the famous Stanley Holloway, such as "Albert and the Lion", but found that the words were so well-known, and because they were poetic and never varied, the audience joined in, and the humour was largely lost. Al Read, though, could be improvised, and his pieces were brief: a married couple's argument over a smell of gas, a bus conductor with an overcrowded bus, a boy embarrassing his Dad by repeating gossip in a barber's shop, and two amateur golfers arguing over their scores, kept the guests quietly attentive and laughing in the right places. They were clearly happy and in good voice.

At the end of that impersonation, Sam said in a low voice, 'Time to get the tea' and Nicky headed for the kitchen, but met Laura just coming down the stairs from the meeting.

'Oh, hello. I'm just going to start the tea,' Nicky told her. 'Everyone's in the laundry lounge; no-one's watching TV. That entertainer is really good. You've missed a treat, but it's not over yet. They're singing again now. The only two not in there are Sid and Mick, and neither of them wants tea.'

'I'll come and help you now,' said Laura. 'I've seen Andy Dodds before. Stella's really worried, though. You'll have to get up there straight after tea break.'

By the time the two carers had done the tea and were carrying it into the laundry lounge, there had been another monologue, and it seemed to be just finishing.

'Oh, this one's good, Nicky,' said Laura. 'I think this is the best of Andy's show. There was an old comedian called Bernard Miles. I say "comedian" but he was really a serious actor – Shakespeare and all that. Anyway, he used to do this act with monologues, as if he was an old country yokel with a drawling accent.

That's why Andy is dressed in that old tunic. It was all about country people who would only drink water from standpipes in the garden and who used to sew each other into their underclothes in the winter and not take baths or anything. Then, at the end, there's a prim-and-proper old lady who tells him off because she said she'd seen his barrow parked outside the local pub and that meant he was inside boozing and she did not approve. He protested that he had left it there only while he was collecting bean sticks, but she did not believe him. So then, later on, he got his barrow and parked it right outside the front door of her cottage. And the audience is all quiet while he repeats it, but then they roar with laughter when he says – "all night"!' There had been a great roar just as Laura and Nicky had started to bring the trays of tea in from the kitchen.

Laura was surprised to see Sam still there, but he said he'd stayed for Andy Dodds, and would take Stella's and Linda's tea up to the office and stay for the meeting with them and with Nicky. He also said that for the last part of his entertainment while the tea was cooling for the guests, Andy would calm the guests down with gentle music. Usually it was "I see the moon, the moon sees me", "As time goes by", "Wonderful, wonderful Copenhagen", and then into romance with "I'll be with you in apple blossom time", and then emotional as well as romantic with "Now is the Hour". They sometimes sang that three times over.

Stella, Linda and Sam had finished their tea by the time Nicky decided to leave Laura to it and rush up the stairs, but she said she didn't want any tea, and so they could get down to the discussion.

'Fine!' said Stella rather abruptly, as she got up from the desk where she had been drinking her tea, and crossed to the armchair so that she could sit centrally to talk to Linda, Sam and Nicky. Nicky had felt a lot of respect for Stella from the moment she met her. In that brief moment of her crossing from the desk to the chair, she tried to look at her objectively. Nicky estimated her age at the late fifties or possibly early sixties. She thought she was slightly younger than Jo, someone else that Nicky thought was impressive, but the two women had many things in common, especially considerable knowledge and experience in medical matters. But there was more than this. There was a calmness, a feeling that both the ladies were on top of things, could cope with anything, would know exactly what to do in any crisis, and would expect those around them to follow their lead.

Stella was by no means stout or portly, but she seemed sturdily built and this strength was added to by the steadiness of her posture. She stood very upright and her head never drooped; it was always held high and she looked forwards. She always looked at you full in the face, straight into your eyes, and her own eyes always seemed steady, focussed, unwavering. Her hair was grey, though not white. There didn't seem to be a parting, and yet the fairly short hair was swept to each side, taken back above each ear, and it stayed neatly in position, always tidy. Her glasses were the same unfussy but functional style: each lens was oval and the supporting titanium metal was thin but clearly evident.

There was nothing unusual about her facial features: eyebrows not noticeable, lips moderately thick and firm, front teeth even and healthily white, with only one or two of them artificial. Her smile, though, was impressive and unforgettable. It emphasised the lines round the edges of her mouth, and down her lower cheeks. She smiled with her eyes, too: deep lines radiated from the corners and from her slightly closed eyes. The lines round her mouth and eye-corners stayed visible all the time: it was as if they assumed their natural position when she smiled and revealed a happy person.

All these impressions had built into a mental picture of Stella each time Nicky had spoken to her this week, and she now found this picture she carried in her mind to be reassuring.

As she sat to face them, her face seemed taut and her cheeks drawn. All three employees were rather nervously expectant.

'All three of you are relatively young,' she began, 'but I expect you have all noticed I have been a bit abrupt and edgy sometimes recently. If you thought I had something on my mind, you were right. I must say I am not alone, and I know many people in the Department of Health and senior medical services have a worry, too. I am sure you will have heard of it. In these days of fast inter-continental travel, there has increasingly been a danger that an epidemic could spread to become global very quickly. That's a pandemic, and I am afraid that it is happening.

'The Chinese government and health service have become aware that a virus, now known as Covid-19, has been emanating from Wuhan, a city in Hubei province in China. A doctor notified the Chinese government of it on Friday 10th January. They suppressed the news for a week but then admitted its existence on Saturday 18th January. Then it began to spread at an alarming speed. Within two weeks, in early February, it had reached a hundred and eleven countries. This speed is breath-taking and terrifying. It's no wonder the authorities are worried.

'We have had pandemics before, but nothing that has travelled as fast as that, not the Asian 'flu of 1957, or SARS and Bird 'flu about ten years ago, or even Ebola, about two years ago. This new virus is not an infectious 'flu or pneumonia like those others. This one is a highly-infectious, multi-organ virus and it is deadly. It is spread from human to human in both infectious and contagious ways. It seems that its speed and deadly nature have left our politicians and Health chiefs uncertain as to what to do. The trouble is that our politicians, like politicians everywhere, tell us only part of the truth. They tell us only as much as they want us to know and they keep letting out bits of information. On March 1st, the Chief Medical officer mentioned victims of the corona virus and spoke of the fact that it was spreading.

'The trouble is that each virus is different from others, and all that the Government's medical advisers can do is concentrate on what they know of previous viruses. A hundred years ago, at the end of the First World War, Spanish 'flu swept through this country and during 1918 and 1919 it killed 200,000 people. Millions were killed worldwide, more than had been killed by the carnage of the War. At that time, the infection was allowed, as they said, to 'move through the country', so that enough people would catch it and recover. All those people would have enough antibodies for them to spread immunity. Unfortunately, the Spanish 'flu took two years to burn itself out and reputable scientists say that you need 60% of the population to have achieved immunity for that to be effective. Therefore, we are talking about hundreds of thousands. That's why at the end of February, the Chief Scientific adviser and Chief Medical officer were jointly forecasting a possible 250,000 deaths.'

Linda and Nicky gasped. 'Wow! That's mighty dangerous, then,' Linda blurted out.

'It is,' continued Stella, 'and I don't think we're being told all the true facts because the Government is afraid that the NHS will be overwhelmed. The Prime Minister has made a speech in which he said, "Many families will lose loved ones." What he didn't say was that the family members they would lose would be their grandparents. Why? Because it is already known that this virus attacks older people rather than young ones. So, let your Granny go for the sake of the others in the family. That means those in care homes like ours, of course, and no-one will be bothered about them. In fact, I think we won't even get a look-in as far as the Government is concerned. In previous viral epidemics, the Government has started giving huge batches of PPE to the NHS. Do you think they'll bother with giving us PPE? Of course they won't. We're not a part of the NHS as far as they're concerned. We're paid for partly by local Councils' Social Care departments and partly by the residents themselves, or totally by the residents, and so we are just a side-line that they don't want to worry about.'

'That's it, then,' volunteered Sam. 'We don't expect any help, and we just soldier on as best we can.'

'No, that isn't all there is to it,' said Stella, sharply. 'We watch what the Government is up to and how it's going to affect us. I think one thing that they will want is for us to continue to take NHS patients as they are discharged. That's what our intermediate patients, or residents, are, though we only have room for two, in these bedrooms upstairs here. The NHS pays us to take them when they're ready to be discharged, so that they don't block beds that they need for newly-infected patients. We don't have those rooms filled at the moment, but just you watch.'

There was then a time when Stella stopped speaking, and the three of them did not know what to say. They just looked down at their hands or stared at the floor. Stella looked round at all three, but none of them would meet her eyes.

'You see, what makes me sure that, in spite of their re-assurances at news conferences, the Government really is confused about what to do, is that they are now saying that they will not have a policy of total suppression of the virus. They will have one of mitigation – that is, they will not wipe it out, but just lessen its effect, just try to control how much of it we can tolerate, just feed some vulnerable people to the virus and hope that the majority of the population will get by. The statisticians call it "flattening the curve" – that is, spread out the number of infections so that you do not have too many at one time. In effect, that's what they did in 1918. But I think that yesterday, March 5th, the Chief Scientist and Chief Medical Officer stepped out of line and got a bit too honest in repeating the possibility of 250,000 deaths, and the politicians and the Prime Minister have got frightened. The Chief Medical Officer has also said this morning that an epidemic is inevitable. The virus has been sweeping across Europe from the East, and suppression is what all their governments are doing to deal with it. They are closing their borders, stopping incoming and outgoing flights at airports, while our Government is talking about "herd immunity". They are trying to suppress it because they are also frightened. They are preventing travel and shutting down industry in Italy and Spain. Some of the stories coming out of Spain are terrifying. The police have found elderly people's care homes abandoned by the staff who have fled and left corpses behind. You cannot believe it.'

Stella looked round quietly at her listeners again, but there was no response, and she resumed. 'Well, the reason I am so stirred up about this is that this morning it has been announced that two deaths from the virus have occurred in England. A family in East Sussex are the first to have been infected in the UK. They must have had it for about two weeks and therefore had it during February. It's started here. Deaths are occurring and they say that an epidemic is inevitable and still they do nothing.'

Stella stopped speaking while she sat quietly, covered her face and rested her elbows in her lap. The three young people continued to look down.

'What are we going to do?' asked Linda, feebly.

'Well, I would normally say that we wait for guidance and instructions from the Department of Health,' said Stella, 'but there is no guidance, no instructions, and they make contradictory statements. Other people that I know in the care industry have told me that they know there are infections in care homes, and everyone is unsure what to do.

'Starting on Monday, I think we will need to discuss ways in which we can isolate our care home to keep the virus out. The trouble is that every day we have tradesmen call with food and other provisions. There are people who service our equipment. All our staff except me live out and come in every day. Visitors to the guests come and go every day. Our guests go out on trips or to the shops in Chignall or Gainsford. They also have appointments at Brookfields, and travel there. We can't stop all these things and carry on living a normal life. But it's a nightmare deciding what to stop in order to minimise the risk of infection. What we are not going to do is to give up.' Here, Stella's eyes bulged and she clenched her fists in a very rare demonstration of passion. 'No. I'm not just going to carry on as if everything is normal, and watch our guests die off one by one, because that is what it will come to. If the Government won't act, then we must decide how to act. I think the Government is just sleepwalking. Well, I'm not going to sleepwalk, and I hope no-one else wants to. I just can't stress enough how serious I think this is.'

Stella lowered her hands again, but only briefly.

'Now, are there any questions any of you want to ask?'

Silence. No response.

'We'll have to think about it, and tell you any ideas we think will help,' said Linda. 'I can't be any more precise until I've thought about it.'

Stella nodded. The other two murmured agreement.

'OK, then,' said Stella, with a sigh and a weak wave of the hand. 'There's nothing unusual happening over the weekend except visitors coming in and out. I don't know if the Church will send anyone to conduct a short service on Sunday morning, if anyone wants one,' she said, without any enthusiasm. 'Linda, you are on each afternoon over the weekend. Nicky, you are here tomorrow afternoon. Then you have Sunday off, but you start at six on Monday and you're on six-to-two all next week. You'll find the mornings are much different from the afternoons. OK?'

'Yes. OK, Stella.' The two girls nodded at Stella's weak smile.

'Right. Nicky, you have to set the supper and finish your shift with Laura today, and Sam, I hope you'll keep feeding us!'

'See you, then,' she said with an air of resignation, as they shuffled out slowly, and went downstairs to digest what Stella had said.

For someone who was normally so controlled and systematic about everything she did and said, all that Stella had just said had tumbled out in rather disorganised profusion. Her three young employees had been a bit surprised. They had some notion of what Stella was going to say, because there had been media coverage of the Covid advance, but it was the fervid vigour of the way she spoke that took them unaware. Stella herself felt a little tired and glad to have got that off her chest, but the person she really wanted to talk to, heart to heart, was Jo – later tonight.

Chapter 5

Stella had left the office door ajar and was waiting for Jo, when she came in through the heavy front door and walked swiftly up the stairs.

Jo Rayner, how glad I am to see you, she thought. I may own and manage this place on my own, and I'm on my own most of the time, but there are times when I long to have someone else as well, to be with, not to lean on but just to be with – a problem shared, and all that. But I don't half need you now, Jo, and I'm glad to have you here.

'Shall we have a cup of tea?' she asked, two seconds after Jo walked in.

'Well, I thought I'd …..'

Stella cut her short. 'It's alright. I've been round with Laura and Nicky, encouraging any guests who needed it, to make their way to their rooms. Everything seems OK. We've switched off the TV in the kitchen lounge, and told them anything else they want, they'll have to watch in their rooms. Laura and Nicky are very good, you know. They've been discreetly looking into each room, asking if they want any help with making a bedtime drink. It's all very gentle, but it's steadily there.' She smiled. 'Those two ladies will be going home now, but I do want to have a drink and a talk with you, Jo. Please.'

Jo knew when Stella really needed her, and she sat down. Stella went into her own sitting room to make the tea. She had already boiled the kettle. She knew there was something deep within herself that felt satisfied now that Jo was in the office. They had both had long and sound experience in nursing and medical matters. Stella felt that Jo's experience of life in general was wider than hers. Stella had never married, just dutifully looked after ageing parents, though, as a qualified nurse, she had seen difficult births, harrowing deaths and everything in between. Jo had experienced all that, too, but Jo had also been married, and had had her own children, Julie and John, who had themselves got married and left her. Her husband, Ken, a ship's captain for a global freight company, really was a man of the world, responsible through all weathers for valuable cargoes and for the lives and safety of his crew, negotiating with aggressive business men in foreign ports, and in her younger days, before the children, Jo had sometimes flown out to meet him for the homeward journey. What a life, but what a friend, too. If there was a person who could cope with anything, it was Jo. Stella carried the tea in, set it down, and looked at Jo with total empathy.

'I've given all six of the others a good talk about the situation we've discussed, Jo, and if they hadn't seen it coming, they know all about it now.'

'The sooner the better,' said Jo. 'I bet they knew anyway.'

'Yes. I dealt with the origin of the virus, the speed of its spread worldwide, the fact that it's infectious and contagious, the theory of "herd immunity", the fact that the old people are the ones the Prime Minister says will be lost, but they won't bother with PPE or anything for us. I told them that the Prime Minister was now saying the Government had moved away from suppression, which is what governments across Europe, especially in Spain and Italy, are doing, and is now aiming for mitigation so that the NHS can cope. Mitigation will spread out the number of infections and deaths, "flattening the curve". He says that in paragraph four of the letter he sent to the whole population. The scientists are frightening everyone by stating the possibility of 250,000 deaths. I said that the really serious thing for us is that the numbers of intermediates will rise everywhere and we'll have some.'

'But we don't have to take those,' interrupted Jo, 'and we haven't had any requests from Brookfields yet, have we?'

'No,' Stella replied quietly, 'but whether or not we do, depends on how our present guests get on. It really will come to that, Jo, and if it is known that we have Covid in Woodside, no other families will want us to have their grannies and grandads. And the point is, we get paid for intermediates.' This was the crux of the care home dilemma. The discussion paused briefly, while the two friends looked steadily into each other's faces.

'Well, did you know this, Stella? I know people elsewhere in caring, and they say the infection is already in care homes, and the proof of what you are saying is that the NHS is said to have block-booked eighteen hundred places in care homes. That will be so that they're ready for when they need them for the intermediates.'

'No.' Stella gave a long sigh. 'I didn't know that, Jo, but it does back up what I've been saying.'

'What did everyone say about that?' Jo asked.

'Very little. I think they were a bit shocked. They said they would have to think about it, and see how they could help.'

There was another pause while most of the tea was drunk.

'You did know about the first two deaths we've had in this country, did you, Jo?'

It was Jo's turn to be rather taken aback. 'No.'

'They lived in East Sussex. The important point to me is if they have now died, they must have had the virus for at least two or three weeks. In other words, they would have had it during February. That's where your news about the infection already spreading to the care homes comes from.'

'Yes. It's no wonder the Medical Officer stands there announcing that an epidemic in this country is inevitable. It's already here.'

'What annoys me beyond measure is that the Government doesn't do anything except talk. Yesterday, the Home Affairs sub-committee heavily criticised them, but it makes no difference. The Prime Minister doesn't do anything except talk. He says we must protect the NHS and that he is "led by the science". He also says we must stay at home and wash our hands. That tells us nothing.'

The two ladies shook their heads and sat in silence again. 'OK then,' continued Stella. 'I also told the other staff the Government were just prevaricating and not acting. I said they were sleep-walking, not aware of how serious things are. I tend to think that the trouble is that the politicians have to keep saying that the NHS will come to our rescue and will cope. I don't think it is ready and I think it has been so starved of money that it doesn't have the resources to cope, and so we have this talk of mitigation, "flattening the curve", anything but say that we must suppress it and lock down like everyone else except Sweden is doing. I suppose the thing is it's so blooming cold in Sweden the virus can't travel through the air. Mind you, Sweden's death rate from Covid is 57 per 100,000, and that is almost the same as Britain, Spain and Italy, and they make visitors to Sweden quarantine when they return.'

'Stella, it is up to us to take a lead. If we say we are not going to sleep-walk like the politicians, what are we going to do?'

'Yes. You're right, Jo. I must tell you that at first I thought I would have regular meetings with all the staff to update them and tell them what strategy we were going to use. But I now think we might need to move more quickly and just tell them facts and tell them to do things.

'Let's do it together, though, Jo. The quickest way to have a meeting is for you and me to phone each other and talk. Shall we have an arrangement that we speak with each other every day by telephone, because you'll only be here when it's your shift, unless there's an emergency?'

'Yes. OK by me.'

'Well, seven each evening would suit me. The guests and carers are then occupied with the evening snack, and I've had my tea, and I'm nearly always in my room, near the phone. Could I suggest that we use the landline phone? Anyone who wants us in an emergency will always use the mobile because they won't know where we are. The kind of contract I have for the landline number here, means that we can have unlimited calls free for up to an hour. So I'll always try to ring you first, though if you want to ring any time, it's up to you.'

'Yes, fine. I have the same kind of contract for my home phone.'

'Right, then.' Stella moved the tea things away for her to deal with later. 'I think the first thing is not to discuss much about procedures and arrangements until we have established with all staff and guests certain information.'

'Yes. I think I know what you're driving at, Stella.'

'The first thing is to get into everyone's head just what this thing is. What are the symptoms if you have the virus? I think that at the first chance I have next week, I'll get them to memorise the symptoms and instruct them always to be on the watch for them in any of the guests, in or out of their rooms, wherever they are. So, do you agree: first, a high temperature – there might be sweating and feverishness, but whether or not, it's the high temperature that can be felt and that we can measure. Second, a dry, persistent cough – the cough is always there. Third, any shortness of breath or difficulty with breathing – that always occurs and the vital symptom of oxygen level in the blood can be checked by me, Kath or you, using the pulse-oxymeter. When we take blood pressure, of course, you, I or Kath will do it. Later, people will feel very tired and lethargic – a great weakness, as with the 'flu. Do you agree that those three, together with that fourth one later, I tell them they must absolutely memorise and look for?'

'Yes, I think that's complete,' said Jo. 'I did hear from a distant relative of mine, that they thought they had it, and they could not taste or smell, and that could be one, but it's never mentioned anywhere else, so we'll leave that for now.'

'Right, then. Early shift Monday, Laura is back again because Linda has done the weekend. Kath is also on early, after you have gone home at six. Nicky's on early for the first time. I will insist that Nicky, Laura, Kath and Sam Wild meet me here sharp at two, and I'll really emphasise as strongly as I can that those symptoms are what they must look out for and then tell you, me or Kath immediately – not at the end of the shift, but the minute they see them. If someone has clear symptoms, it will be serious for us, and we'll have to decide where they go and how we look after them. Then, straight after two, I get onto Linda and Maggie. I'll do at least the Monday, Tuesday and Wednesday all-nighters next week, Jo, and you can rest a bit, but I'll be on the phone if there's anything for you to know.'

'OK, Stella. Any procedures necessary, like isolating people and banning visitors, no trips and no going into Chignall or Gainsford we'll sort out a bit later.'

'Yes. One thing, though. There was a shopping centre trip going to Nottingham on Tuesday. With Easter just three and a half weeks away from then, a number will want to go, but I think I'll cancel that now, because it's a big city and a cancellation of anything and giving the reasons why will impress on people that there is something going on, and that we are serious about it. So thanks, Jo. You'll need to walk round and tuck a few in bed from now on. See you later.'

There was one matter that occurred to Stella over the weekend which had not been mentioned in her talk with Jo, and that was the question of face masks to be worn when nurses or carers had close personal contact with guests. This would nearly always occur in the morning before breakfast, in respect of the administration of any medication or help with washing or dressing. In her telephone call to Jo at 7 pm on Saturday, Stella pointed out that this would occur with May, with her Levoxyl tablet for thyroid deficiency. It didn't arise with asthma, where the three guests concerned, Chris, May and Marsha, always related to their consultants at Brookfields. It did arise, though, with the diabetics and their metformin tablets for Lorna, Lew, Dennis and June. It also was relevant to the guests with weak hearts, Margery and Mick, with their warfarin, and Martin and Matt with their beta-blockers.

Jo agreed that all the appropriate nurses and carers might as well begin to put on masks when they went in these people's rooms with medication in the mornings, and also if and when they had to help them with washing or dressing in the morning, as might happen with Margery, Ella, Maurice and Sid. Jo pointed out that there had been no special guidance or instructions from the Department of Health yet, but if the policy was to alert people to necessary procedures, and impress on them that dangerous conditions were actually present, then they might as well start early and promptly and strictly, as she, Stella, was already doing by cancelling the trip to Nottingham on Tuesday.

There was, therefore, prompt agreement and a reassuring exchange of promises that they would support each other.

'I've got a couple of things to give you, Nicky,' said Kath, as soon as Nicky had come with springy steps up the staircase and into the office very early, six o' clock, on Monday morning. Nicky was glad that she lived not far away along Woodside Avenue. 'Laura's beaten you to it this morning, so I've already given hers to her. We have time to go through this because breakfast for guests doesn't start until seven. First, here's a list of Covid symptoms that I want you to read through now and commit to memory. You'll see that there are three main symptoms, the high temperature, the cough and the breathing difficulty.' Kath paused a few seconds and watched Nicky as she was reading. 'Don't worry about the oxygen levels and the tiredness for the moment – just get the main three really fixed in your mind and keep thinking about them all the time you are at work. Now, I want you to promise me that each time you see or speak to or come into contact with any of our guests at any time, you will consciously ask yourself whether they have any of these symptoms. If they do, you must tell Stella or me or Jo, whichever one of us you see first, immediately. OK?' As Nicky nodded, Kath moved swiftly from "stern lecture" mode to "smiling and friendly" mode. 'I'm carrying mine in the front pocket of my uniform,' she said. Nicky folded her paper and did the same.

'Oh, this will be what Stella was talking about on Friday afternoon. It's a bit sudden, isn't it?' she asked, in all innocence.

'It's here, Nicky,' said Kath, emphatically. 'Stella wasn't talking about something theoretical, something in the future. It's here, and it's here now. We've got to be vigilant and on the watch for it everywhere. The situation is deadly serious.' There was another pause. 'Now, here's the second little present for you, a face mask. Just try it on. Loop it right over your head so that the elastic is round the back of your neck. You need to have it covering your mouth and nose when you come close to any guest, even when you're speaking with them. You can keep your distance when you're speaking to them or when you're serving them in the dining room, but when you're giving them something, helping them to wash or dress in the mornings, then, on those occasions, make sure you pull up the mask to cover your mouth and nose. The rest of the time, you can let it slip down under your chin: that's why it's held in place round your neck, OK?' Kath did not wait for a comment or answer, but rushed on. 'Now, I've told Laura that I want you to come with me as I go round the rooms first thing this morning, so that you get to know how we have to look after the guests each morning by giving them whatever medication they need, if any, and just keep an eye out to see whether they need any help in getting out of bed, or dressing or washing. The beginning of each day is quite critical with elderly people. If they have any weakness or illness, that's when it will take effect.'

While Kath was talking, Nicky had slipped the elastic of the mask over her head, and tried it for fit over her nose and mouth. It seemed perfect, and Nicky smiled her relief.

'OK, then. Lead on,' she said, with all the good humour she could muster. The two ladies went quickly down the staircase, through the laundry lounge, and then through the laundry itself – so cold and still and deserted without Maggie's warmth and energy.

'I've collected all the tablets we'll need from those casement cupboards in the office. You'll have found out by now they're always kept locked.'

Nicky soon got used to Kath's routine, as they progressed into the corridor and Kath gave a soft knock on the first door. She pushed it open gently. 'Good morning, Vic,' – it was just a gentle call, nothing noisy, nothing sudden. Kath waited for a reply and got a grunt from Vic: 'Yes. Good morning.' She explained to Nicky that if she didn't get a reply after a suitable lapse of time, she called softly again, and put the light on if there was still no reply.

'I only need the light on for two or three seconds, and I can tell immediately if there's anything wrong,' she explained. 'They have to answer the second time, because if they don't, I keep the light on until they do.'

'Oh, another thing,' said Kath after she had looked into Jane's room, 'we encourage them not to lock their doors at night, but if they do, I've got my bunch of master keys, and I use it!'

'Now here's the first one to be careful with,' continued Kath, as she approached Margery's door. 'Wait until you're sure she's well and truly awake before you ask if she's OK, and if she needs any help. That will be with dressing and showering, or even just getting out of bed, because you will have noticed by now that Margery has a weight problem and a weak heart. She is also one who has fallen down in the past, and can't get up on her own. This warfarin that I'm giving her is the gentlest treatment for a suspect heart. You can't do anything suddenly with Margery.'

Kath and Nicky put on their masks when they went into Margery, and got a puzzled look, but no comment. For this morning at least, everything went smoothly with her, and there seemed to be no problem. Nicky already knew that the next guest along, Martin, had a weak heart, but he was more robust in his general health than Margery, and had been prescribed beta-blockers.

There was nothing to delay them with Martin, but Ella was a much different matter. 'Ella probably has Lewy Body dementia,' said Kath. 'That's why she can't remember things. You have to take the lead with her,' she advised Nicky. 'You decide what she will be wearing, and while you're talking to her, you get out the underclothes, tights and her dress for the day, and lay them on the bed. She'll go straight to them and put them on after you've been looking after her in the shower. In the shower itself, ask if she wants a rubber cap on, but assume that she does and put it on for her. Then put her bath towel ready and after you have turned the shower on and adjusted the temperature to what you think she'll like, invite her to go in. She'll know how to wash herself once she's in, so come away but don't leave the en-suite. When she's pulled the door and walked out, you turn it off for her. A quick turn as far as it will go anti-clockwise is all you'll need, and she will probably grab and use the bath towel while you are switching off. Give her plenty of time, because, fortunately, she's very fussy about getting herself completely dry. Once she's decided she's finished, take her bath-hat off, open the door and she'll go straight to the clothes you've put ready and put them on very quickly and without any dithering or any fuss. Make sure she has a box of tissues, and wipe her nose if it needs it: after the first time, she may well remember that herself, but I feel sorry for her because of the trouble she has with her mucus. She's usually perfectly happy afterwards and goes off to breakfast in a good humour. Sometimes Barbara, her friend next door, will have come in or be waiting for her, but if not, off she goes. You'd better put your mask on, Nicky, come in and watch me go through all that, and I'll leave it to you tomorrow, but I'll be somewhere near, because I will have had to give her the Levodopa tablet before anything else.

'Barbara, next door, moans and complains a lot. She doesn't need anything from us, though, and she really is good the way she looks out for Ella and keeps her safe.

'Lorna, room seven, needs no special attention, apart from the metformin tablet, but to save time, let's make sure she takes that first, and then we'll leave her to get on with everything, and make sure that Maurice, next door, is up and about. Be careful to ask Maurice if he's having a shower, and if he is, fuss around in his room while he's in there. I can't remember him giving any trouble, but he doesn't walk well and could easily trip or slip. If that ever does happen, just go straight in, turn off the water and then go and push the bedside button to activate a nurse's pager. Especially in wet conditions, don't try to manage him on your own if he falls.'

Maurice decided he didn't want a shower today, and asked why they were wearing masks, but they quickly moved on, stopping to give Lew his metformin and Mick his warfarin. Chris was in good voice, and Matt, in number twelve, had his beta-blocker. The happy one was May. She was already up, dressed and singing. She called out to Kath before she opened the door to her, calling her 'my darling,' holding her hand out for the Levoxyl, promising she would beat her to the dining room and saying she would wear a mask, too. Sid needed help with washing only in the sense of having it suggested that he might at least wash his face and hands, because he never seemed keen on applying water to himself, only to his plants. One other suggestion he sometimes needed was that it was not a good idea to go for his breakfast in the dining room with his gardening boots on: a portion of good humour usually got him through the day. Dennis in number fifteen and June in number seventeen, also needed their metformin, but apart from that, Kath and Nicky moved quickly along the far corridor to the end. There were plenty of hard looks at the masks, but no more comment.

'Now you've watched me check each room, Nicky, and when you're on duty on your own, you do the same to check that the guests are awake and moving about, but don't worry about the various pills you've seen me handing out. In fact, you ignore them and leave that to Stella, Jo or me. You just need to keep a special lookout for Margery, Ella, Maurice and Sid. By all means, ask everyone if they're alright and if they need anything. If they've got a problem, you can't be expected to know about it unless they tell you, but you will find they're not backward in coming forward and telling you if anything is wrong. Some will enjoy talking about it.'

By now, they had walked back to the central part of the building, and Nicky could tell that Kath was wanting to go up to the office, and so she would go to serve at breakfast on her own.

'Remember that you do the fetching and carrying, Nicky, so that we don't have any falls or collisions or spillages, and that includes the tea or coffee at the end. As far as allergies are concerned, there are only two people to bear in mind. Don't say anything to Margery about her weight because she might consider it offensive. If she needs anything clinical to be pointed out, it's best to leave that to Stella. Then there's Barbara and Lorna. Barbara cannot possibly come into contact with nuts in our kitchen, and I think she'll remember to steer clear of any kind of fish. We need to be careful, though, of Lorna and what cereal she might ask for at breakfast. She can have no cereal containing wheat, barley or oats – and that's most of them. She cannot have any ordinary toast or bread, though Ryvita or gluten-free bread or anything containing rice are OK. Rice Krispies or Rice

Snaps are the obvious answer and there is a special porridge which Sam Wild keeps in stock. If she remembers, she should ask Sam specially for that if she is going to want it. Ordinary porridge, by the way, is very popular with everyone else. It's the only thing Sam serves hot every day of the week, and it nearly all goes. Mind you, Sam is very good at cooking it. And, I must say, if they want shredded wheat, it is always the old form, the biscuit, that they want, and very rarely the bite-size varieties. Sam puts out plenty of fruit and fruit juice, and if you can encourage them to have any, I would do. Anyway, as far as Lorna is concerned, you will find that Chris nearly always sits with her, and will be very quick to intervene if she asks for something she shouldn't have. Trust him. He knows better than she does what she can have.' With a smile and a chuckle about that, Kath quickly mounted the stairs, and Nicky went on through the kitchen lounge and into the dining room. As no-one else would be able to wear a mask in the dining room, Nicky removed hers and put it in the pocket of her apron.

All the tables had been set by Sam with jugs of milk for cereals or porridge or tea, sugar and butter and jam or marmalade for toast. Orange juice and apple juice were both very popular in equal measure, and Nicky rather enjoyed whizzing round with trays of glasses, and setting them down on the tables. Sam had two electric boilers always on the go with hot water for tea, and it was invariably served as a pot for two. There were two tables for four, and the most convenient thing for the carer was if the tea-drinkers all sat at those tables, so that was eight catered for quickly, and one pot could go for two tea-drinkers on any small table. There were, though, calls for a number of coffees which had to be obtained individually from a machine that was like a vending machine without needing money. Nicky was relieved to see that Barbara and Ella sat together at a small table.

Kath was right about the porridge. As it was still only the middle of March, Sam had a big tureen of it constantly heated. Many journeys with dishfuls kept Nicky on the go. Barbara and Lorna (with Chris's approval) had their own gluten-free version, coming from an ordinary pan on Sam's hob. Modern, sugary cereals were not, Nicky found, very popular, except for Frosties, and Weetabix seemed to be preferred to Shredded wheat. Bananas were the most popular fruit, though there was a variety available: oranges, apples, grapes and olives. Apart from the porridge, nothing was cooked, though Nicky had already heard that tomorrow was the day for cooked breakfasts, and so was Sunday. Tuesday was the one day in the week for cooked breakfasts because if guests were going for the day's outing, that could be thought of as a special day, too. Hot breakfast options made those two days of the week special.

Sunday breakfast had hot choices of eggs fried, boiled or scrambled, bacon, baked beans, black pudding, and fried potatoes. Stella had pointed out to Nicky that breakfast was later on Sunday at 8.30 and some guests liked to think of it as a different, if not special, day.

About half a dozen people went out to morning service in the Chignall church, and for those not so mobile, someone from the church came and conducted a simple, half-hour service during the afternoon in the laundry lounge. The local vicar had pointed out that communion could be brought to anyone on request, but that was rare, with Sunday services available as well.

Today though, Monday, it was the normal cold breakfast with warm porridge. All that was available was set out as though it was a buffet, though the guests asked for what they wanted and remained seated while the carer, and sometimes the nurse as well, served them.

Once the eating and the tea or coffee was finished with, guests drifted off to their rooms in twos or threes. After the clearing away and wiping of the tables was completed, Nicky helped Sam with the washing of the plates and dishes, and wiping and drying, so that he could get on with his next major event, lunch, the biggest meal of the day, always freshly cooked.

Nicky then set off on a tour of the rooms and lounges to see what help the guests might need, and to keep an eye on what they were doing. It had to be quick, and similar to early afternoon: bed-making if not done or bed-changing if it was the day for it; use of the large push vacuum cleaner and the small, hand-held one; a general tidy round; the en-suite, once teeth-cleaning, showering and any necessary shaving had been done, had to be cleaned and wiped down all through, the washbasin thoroughly washed, face flannels and toothbrushes arranged and towels replaced if necessary.

For the guests, every morning was the same except for those who might go out on a trip for the day. Otherwise, guests stayed in their rooms doing their own tasks or following their interests. There was TV in every room, though they were not much used in the mornings. Most people at some time walked into the village of Chignall. There was a petrol station with a convenience store, which sold snacks from the shelf, sweets and cigarettes, though any smokers could indulge the habit only outside Woodside Lodge. What did sell, though, were daily newspapers, and many guests, having walked there and bought a paper, took it back to the Lodge and spent most of the morning reading it. There was also a pharmacy and a lending library in the village, open three days a week, and about a third of the guests used it. At the other end of the village from the Lodge there was a public park, which was very well organised and arranged in hedges, paths and flower-beds. It had many seats and was very popular, especially in the summer. To the park and back for lunch was a popular way of spending many mornings for those who liked a more substantial walk. Most guests made their own arrangements for hairdressing at a salon in Chignall, though there was a visiting one at the Lodge for those who preferred that.

So the morning tended to be busy with much bustling about and a variety of individual or paired activities. Sometimes, Nicky worked with Laura on room-cleaning or tidying out waste, but at other times she just went and tended to things when she saw a need. Laura had told Nicky that morning routines were always the same, except for occasional days out on Tuesdays, and if there was an unusual interruption, it was medical and was referred to the duty nurse, and some guests might need to be taken to the local surgery in the Lodge's minibus, which was also done by the nurse.

At about half-past eleven, the two carers went to lay the dining room tables for lunch. Sam had prepared and organised the evening snack by this time and he left that covered and ready while he prepared the lunch. Nicky looked through Sam's menus for the forthcoming days, and she saw that what he had planned was a series of simple, plain, nutritious meals that would be familiar and popular with people of the age of the guests. The starter was always soup.

Today was a little sparse compared to most days: chips and chipolata sausages, with baked beans, but there was apple pie and custard, which was one of Sam's most popular puddings. Other than that, on different days there were kedgeree, gluten-free pizza, hunter's chicken with vegetables (carrots, broccoli and parsnips), toad-in-the-hole, chops with potatoes and vegetables, and mixed grill: bacon, fried eggs, mushrooms, fried tomatoes, black pudding. Sweet courses were ice cream, sticky toffee pudding, apple pie and custard, steamed pudding with custard, dumpling and syrup: some of these were marked as not recommended for anyone with diabetes! Meals were always concluded with a choice of tea (by the pot) or coffee (from the machine).

Lunch started promptly at 12.30, even a little before, and usually carried on until two o' clock. It was very busy, and the duty nurse, usually Kath and sometimes Stella as well, helped with all the fetching and carrying. Laura pointed out that it was 'all hands on deck' for clearing away and washing and cleaning afterwards because if you stayed after two, there was always plenty of left-overs which you could eat in the kitchen that were probably better than you would prepare for yourself at home. Certainly, Sam sampled his own work at the end.

Nicky therefore felt full and satisfied by the time she had cleared the dining room and went up to the office to collect her things to go home. She was in time to hear Stella telling Linda that she wanted to see her, Sam and Maggie in the office before she, Linda, gave out the jigsaws for the afternoon. She was saying that she had something to give them and tell them before the afternoon started. Nicky knew what that was.

Chapter 6

Nicky was on the early shift, six-till-two, all week. She served the hot breakfast option as well as the rest of what was on offer on Tuesday, although the Nottingham shopping centre trip had been cancelled by Stella at the end of the week before. As Laura had told her, all mornings were much the same, and always very busy. The two carers worked hard to keep the breakfasts going, while visiting the rooms before seven, following on after Kath had taken in the various medications. For the first three days, Stella was around as well, because she had taken over the all-nighters from Jo on the Sunday night. She always wanted to discuss something with Kath when she came on duty at six, and both the nurses came and helped with the breakfasts. Nicky was especially glad of their help when the hot breakfast option was available at seven.

The only time there was much change to routine was if someone was not feeling well when they woke up. This happened with Margery on the Tuesday morning, and the carers were glad to leave Stella and Kath, wearing their masks, to get her out of bed, showered and dressed, and when she passed by the open door, Nicky spotted them taking her blood pressure readings. She appeared later at breakfast, so there could not have been much wrong.

Everybody must have been following the news of the day, on TV bulletins or the news channels or the regular headlines on the radio. There was a Cobra (Cabinet Office Back Room) meeting on Thursday 12th March, after which the Government announced that they were moving from the "containment" phase of dealing with Covid-19 to the "delay" phase. What they were wanting to delay was the peak on the graphs showing the number of infectious patients admitted to hospital and how many positive tests and subsequent deaths that were being recorded. They wanted the delay in order to "flatten the curve" of infections so that the NHS would not be overwhelmed. The news bulletins spoke of heavy criticism of the Department of Health and Social Services by the Home Affairs sub-committee in the Houses of Parliament.

The Prime Minister had also begun a series of daily filmed news conferences with a small "socially-distanced" audience at No. 10 Downing Street. At these conferences, the Prime Minister was flanked by the Government's Chief Scientific Adviser and the Chief Medical Officer. There was another one of these on Friday 13th March, when people were told to self-isolate with their families if they showed any of the symptoms of a high temperature, a persistent cough or difficulties with breathing and a shortness of breath. People with these symptoms were also told to telephone the NHS on 111. It was also announced that many international events had been abandoned and all public sporting events were to be cancelled.

By that Friday, Jo Rayner was back on night shift, but as soon as she arrived at 9pm, she and Stella had another one of their talks in the office before Jo went round to check on the guests.

'What's irritating me, Jo, is that there's been no change, nothing definite, nothing clear,' Stella said, as she placed Jo's tea next to her. "Some sporting events will have to be cancelled," they say. "We are trying to delay the virus. You must self-isolate if you have any symptoms, and ring 111, and keep washing your hands." Oh, I am sick of this shilly-shallying, of wanting to have it both ways. All across Europe, they're stopping air travel, shutting down industry, and we just tell people to wash their hands and look for symptoms.'

'I'm not sure that they're correct in their list of symptoms,' said Jo. 'I have heard from another source, a relative who wouldn't try to mislead me, that he has not been able to smell or taste for days. He is not imagining it; he's sure of it. He's not been tested but he did ring 111, and they were absolutely adamant, he said: if he had not got a high temperature, he had not got it.'

'Yes. I suppose all we can do at present is what we've already done: tell the staff to keep looking for symptoms, and wearing masks for close contact.'

'There's also been mention of having it asymptomatically, and therefore not knowing.'

'Yes. Oh well, we won't stop visiting this weekend, but there's supposed to be another Cobra meeting on Monday, so we'll think again then.'

It was an uneventful weekend in which many of the guests had visitors and there was a number of groups walking round Chignall or the grounds of the Lodge. Monday 16th March was equally uneventful and quite predictable in spite of the fact that there was a Cobra meeting. A statement afterwards gave little that was new: people were advised to self-isolate if they noticed any symptoms. In the case of Woodside, they were to tell Stella or Jo or Kath. The Government statement also said there were to be no unnecessary social contacts and no non-essential travel.

The following day, Tuesday, however, there were some surprising statements before the news conference. In order to combat the expected severe economic downturn, the Chancellor announced many loans and financial assistance to companies large and small, amounting to 330 billion pounds. This would be unprecedented in peacetime. It included a scheme whereby the Government would pay 80% of the wages or salaries of all employees who could not work from home and whose companies had to close down during the pandemic which was coming. This meant those employees could be furloughed, instead of made redundant and therefore unemployed. There was also a scheme to pay self-employed people who could not work or who had been told not to work, although there would be an administrative delay of some months before payment could be made.

However, as Stella emphatically pointed out to Jo, the Government was still not closing our borders and there was still no general lockdown. Another strange action taken was that restrictions on airports were actually lifted, in spite of the fact that foreign airports and airlines were doing the opposite.

Ominous events on the following day, Wednesday 18th March, were that Italy and France announced a total lockdown of their countries and indeed all European union countries closed their borders. Ryan Air and British Airways grounded all their aeroplanes for the foreseeable future and in Britain all schools were to close indefinitely from Friday 20th March.

On Thursday 19th March, the respective bodies concerned cancelled the Oxford and Cambridge University boat race, and the Grand National at Aintree was also cancelled. Apparently, they had both made that decision on Tuesday 17th but not announced it until the Thursday. 'Yes, but would you believe,' Jo said in her 7pm phone call to Stella, 'there was a European football match in Liverpool on Monday night, with its huge crowd, and the Cheltenham horse-racing has been allowed to go on all week. All week! He won't let that lot be deprived of their pleasure.'

'Yes, Jo, I don't think we have a choice,' said Stella, when Jo arrived for the night shift. 'I think we have to lock down. The man in charge of our country might be shilly-shallying and afraid to make a decision, but I'm not. I'm about saving lives and keeping this whole place safe, not putting it all at risk.' She leaned towards her friend and colleague. 'Are you with me, Jo?'

'Yes,' said Jo. 'I'm with you all the way. I'll just go out and make one round of the rooms to check, and then I'll come back and together we can make our plans.' She turned to give Stella a weak smile as she was leaving, and as Stella watched her receding back, not for the first time she thought how much she admired Jo Rayner.

Jo was back in fifteen minutes, and was smiling as she came into the office. 'I think everyone's happy,' she said, in a cheerful tone that belied her true mood. She was in total agreement with Stella.

'Let's make a list of the things we'll have to do and plan,' Stella said with a sigh and with pen and pad at the ready. 'We're about to start a weekend that sees a higher proportion of visitors than during the week. I said before you went out, Jo, that a day, never mind a weekend, could be critical, might eventually be the difference between someone living and dying. So I think the first urgent thing is to stop those visitors coming in. Do you agree?'

'It seems harsh and it seems abrupt and sudden,' said Jo, and she could see Stella open her mouth to argue the point, but stopped her by raising her hand and waving it at her. 'Yes. I know. These are harsh times. It's not a game we're playing; it's deadly serious and we have to fight. Yes, I agree, Stella, but I think that that's one thing we need to be gentle and diplomatic about.'

'Yes. Well, I'm going to put the work in on that one. After you've gone home in the morning to think about what we're deciding now, I'll phone Kath at home, because she's off until Monday, and I'm doing the weekend mornings. I'll also leave her to think it over and ask her to ring me back over the weekend if she has any worries or misgivings. If either you or Kath have any serious reservations about anything proposed, then I'll have to seriously think again, and we'll see what arrangements we can make. So, for the moment, I'll assume that the first thing we've got to stop if we're going to isolate is the number of people going in and out. On that assumption, then, I'll go round all the rooms after breakfast tomorrow and tell everyone individually that we are stopping all visiting forthwith, starting tomorrow so that each guest can phone potential visitors and tell them, and give them the option of phoning me back during the morning or at any other time. Yes, that might be the hardest and most time-consuming thing we have to do, Jo, and I think it's right that I should do it straightaway.'

Jo nodded. 'Yes. I agree with that.'

'Right. The next thing, then, is what we have delivered here each day. Sometimes, Sam goes and finds what he wants in Gainsford, especially the meat, but for most of the food, he gives an order online and it is delivered. I think I'd better tell him to order everything online, and when it arrives, he had better put it aside for a period of time before using it. Thankfully, we do all our own laundry, but I'll tell Maggie that any new bedlinen must be ordered online and only she deals with it when it comes.' There was a pause for thought for a few moments before Stella resumed: 'Just as we don't want anyone coming in, we'll have to tell all the guests that they can't go out either. Whatever it is, shopping, visiting family, anything, they just cannot go. Our minibus will be thoroughly sanitised, and only you or I, Jo, take anyone to the surgery or Brookfields in Gainsford, and they sanitise their hands and any possessions on return. As far as our life in the Lodge is concerned, guests can go only in the grounds, no further, and even there, if they meet anyone, they keep their distance. We can't have any trips out on Tuesdays, and no music and movement, or any other entertainment on Wednesdays or Fridays. Inside the building, we all count as one family. We can't very well wear masks in the dining room or when we're near people we live with all the time, and all mail will have to be quarantined for two days. I'm sure our kitchen hygiene is well up to scratch anyway.'

'Well, that's all about what guests can't do. What about what they can?' asked Jo.

'I think we'll have to explain that everyone can mix freely within the building, and the same goes for everything we have to touch,' continued Stella. 'It's just that anything that's imported, so to speak, must be put aside for a while and sanitised if possible. We'll have to put sanitiser dispensers around everywhere, including in all the rooms.'

'Yes. That still leaves us with one big and serious problem, though, doesn't it?' said Jo.

There was a long, silent pause.

'Yes. I know what you mean, Jo. The staff. Everyone except me lives somewhere else, and comes in and goes out each day.'

They looked at each other, and there was another long pause.

'I'll make it easy for you, Stella,' said Jo, eventually. 'There's only one way to do it, isn't there?' Stella nodded. 'We, or as many of us as can, will have to move in and live with the guests, like you do.'

'Yes.' Stella took the conversation along. 'Not everybody will be able to. They live in families and they have responsibilities to them. Well, then, I'll have to explain to everyone in groups, and leave them to decide, each one for themselves. Tomorrow is Saturday, so it will be Laura and Kath on in the morning. I'll ask to see them at two o' clock, and I'll ask Sam to stay for a few minutes at that time, too. It's Linda in the afternoon because Nicky's having the weekend off, and I'll see Linda and Maggie at an extended cup-of-tea time in the afternoon. I'll explain the situation to them all, ask them to think about whether they can live in, and to let me know on Monday. As Linda will not be in on

Monday, I'll ask her to ring me on Monday with her decision. I'll phone Nicky at home, explain everything, and ask her to let me know some time on Monday when she's here. And perhaps you can let me know your decision tomorrow night, Jo.'

'Yes, fair enough. I'll have to speak to Ken about it, of course. As luck would have it, he is back in this country at the moment, but he's in port in Southampton and we talk on the phone. I won't see him back in Chignall until Tuesday, but I'll make up my mind after speaking to him some time tomorrow.'

'We'll leave it at that, then,' said Stella, 'unless there's anything else you need to ask about and we can discuss.'

Jo shook her head, and Stella made her way back to her own lounge.

'See you in the morning.'

Stella was very pleased with the way Nicky had been learning and working for the three weeks she had now worked at the Lodge. She decided that she would let her have a good night's sleep before she phoned her on Saturday morning, March 21st, to explain the situation.

When Stella did telephone Nicky at home, she listened quietly and attentively while Stella outlined the political and medical situations, and what the implications were for the population in general, and Woodside Lodge in particular. She moved on to the decision to isolate the Lodge and the restrictive arrangements that involved. Finally, she came to the choice each member of the staff would have to make for themselves because the whole situation meant that they would have to isolate, too. In answer to questions, Stella promised that she would pay the staff who did not want to move into the Lodge, until the Government's furlough scheme got moving, and she also told Nicky she could have until Monday at two o' clock, when she came on duty, to give her answer.

Stella explained everything to Laura, Kath and Sam at two o' clock that day, Saturday, and Linda and Maggie at three o' clock. She asked if all of them would give their final answer on Monday. Linda, as she was not on duty, would have to phone her some time on Monday.

At nine o' clock that evening, Jo arrived to tell Stella that she had discussed it at length on the phone with Ken, who had agreed that, as he would be away again by the end of the week, he had no objection to her living at the Lodge. In fact, he said he admired her bravery. Jo added, though, that she would like Stella to do night duty on Sunday, and let her and Ken have the Monday together so that she would move in on Tuesday morning. Stella looked as if a great weight had been taken from her shoulders. She walked across the office to Jo, who stood up and the two friends embraced and held each other firmly for some moments.

'Thank you, Jo,' breathed Stella as they pulled apart. 'I think you are brave, too – and loving and loyal, of course, but brave, too.' Stella told Jo that she hadn't slept much on the Friday night, but she probably would do now, Saturday, and would do the all-nighter on Sunday. She also said that she thought it couldn't be done without Sam and Maggie agreeing, as well as Jo. She thought, though, that as they both lived on their own and had no dependants, there was a good chance they might agree. If they did, then she had calculated that if one more person agreed, it could be done. She told Jo that she just daren't anticipate people's answers, and just left it to them and their conscience.

Stella did indeed sleep well on Saturday night, and was up early to help Kath with the medication and Laura with the breakfasts. Sunday seemed to her a strangely quiet day without the usual visitors in the afternoon. She felt calm and quiet in her mind, too, because she had made her decision, Jo had agreed to stand with her, everyone else had been told and asked for their decision, and she was just waiting for Monday. Then, depending on what the staff told her, she would know whether she could do this thing she had planned, or whether she would just have to wait, like a helpless victim, for the virus to strike her and all those people for whom she was responsible. That, she did not want to contemplate.

Kath did not want to wait until the end of her shift to give Stella her answer on Monday morning, 23rd March. She had collected all the medicines she needed as she began her morning's work at 6am. She had called in at the nine rooms on the first corridor, when just as she turned the corner to the second corridor, she saw Stella hurrying to catch her up.

'I'll have to tell you that I've decided I can't live in, when you arrange that, Stella,' she said, before Stella could speak. 'I discussed it with my husband last night, and we both agreed it was out of the question. I have two school – age children, nine and twelve. We don't know what's going to happen with the schools, whether I will have to have them at home, but even if they're at school, I've got to look after them all and I can't risk taking an infection back into the family. I can't just leave them.'

'That's fine, Kath, absolutely fine,' said Stella, quickly. 'I quite understand that it's a lot to ask, apart from the danger to the staff themselves, and you have to have your priorities. I will keep your job open, and pay you anyway.' She smiled to reassure Kath.

'Thank you for that, but I don't know if I could take the money, Stella.'

'Yes. Please do. It will keep your job open for you, and the Government will end up paying most of it.'

Kath stroked her forehead, with a feeling of relief. 'Thank you, then, Stella. You are so good. I do appreciate it.'

Laura was following along the first corridor. 'I'm sorry, Stella,' she began, without being asked. 'I'm still only twenty-eight, and I have two young children. My family has to be my priority.'

'That's rather what I expected,' said Stella, reassuringly. 'Of course your family comes first. They need you. I'll keep your job open, and you'll be paid.'

'Thank you, Stella,' said Laura, so full of feeling that she could say no more and continued down the corridor.

That's two down, thought Stella, and now I'll see Sam, Maggie and Nicky at two o' clock.

After the phone call from Stella on Saturday morning, Nicky thought about the problem and decided to mention the topic to all the family on Saturday evening. She needed to know their opinions about it, and also whether they could foresee any problems that she couldn't, or could think of any factors of the situation that had not occurred to her.

They had eaten a mixed grill, as they usually did on a Saturday evening, after Yvonne, mother of Sean and Nicky, had come home at six, when the Co-op in Chignall, where she worked, closed. This was a fairly quick and easy meal to prepare and cook, and so Sean had volunteered to cook it, as he usually did.

'Oh, that was good, Sean. Thank you,' said Nicky. 'I'll wash up and clean the grill pan in a few minutes, but while we're all here together, I want to tell you about something that's going on at work at the Lodge.' The rest of the family looked at her expectantly. She had been excited and full of a bubbly enthusiasm the first week she had worked at the Lodge, but had not said much since then, saying it was all settling down into a routine for her, and she had to get up very early to be there for six o' clock when she was on early shift.

'You know that Stella Holden owns it and is in charge of everything. Well, she has been talking to the staff during today, and she phoned me this morning because I've got the weekend off. She said that there was a lot of worry about the spread across Europe of this corona virus, and the Prime Minister is having news conferences and all that. He has said the pubs, clubs and restaurants have got to close. Italy and France have closed their borders, all the aeroplanes are grounded and sports events have been cancelled. Even the schools closed yesterday.'

'Yes. We've finished early because it's Easter in three weeks,' agreed Sean, who was in the Lower Sixth. 'I can't go back until they've got in touch with me and told me when.'

'Right,' continued Nicky. 'Stella Holden thinks it's only a matter of time before the whole country shuts down, as they have done in Italy and France. She says she doesn't know why the Prime Minister has not announced it, as they have been doing all through Europe, and people aren't allowed to travel anywhere else anyway. But she also says any day lost is a day allowing the virus to rage on. All the elderly people in the Lodge are vulnerable because, it seems, the virus mostly attacks the old because their immune system can't cope with it. Instead of just waiting for the virus to come, she's going to close the Lodge down and isolate it to keep the virus out. So, there are going to be no more trips out, as there often are on Tuesdays, no more entertainments in the afternoons as there are on Wednesdays and Fridays. The chef has to order all food online and have it delivered. There will be no visitors, and the guests can't go out into Chignall or anywhere else and they can only go to a doctor's appointment in our minibus. But, she says that in order to isolate properly, the staff can't go in or out either. That means they either do not go to work any more until they're told they can, or they will have to move into the Lodge and live there with the old people. She says everyone has to make up their own mind by Monday morning, and she'll keep their job open if they don't want to go in.

'What do you think I should do?'

'Wow! It'll be mighty risky to live all the time with the old ones,' said Sean.

'Looks as if it will be mighty risky if I don't go in, as well,' said Nicky.

'What about pay?' asked John, her father.

'Oh, I forgot to say. She says she'll pay us, and keep the job open.'

'Can you take precautions?' asked Yvonne.

'There might be some protective clothing if we have enough, but there's no immunisation of any kind, no vaccine or anything.'

There followed a short silence, while they all looked at their plates and considered this new problem for Nicky.

'Well, what's she going to do if no-one will live in, or if only one or two will live in?' asked Sean.

'That's the worst of the problem,' said Nicky. 'She would have to close.'

'What about the residents?'

'Find them somewhere else to go, or they might have to go back to their families.'

'Well, I don't think it's worth it,' said Sean, the most talkative and impulsive person round the table. 'If you move in, you risk the near certainty of catching Covid, which can be fatal. If you are going to get paid if you don't go, why should you? Look after yourself and take the money, I say.'

'Yes. That's what I would say I think,' said John. 'If you stay out, you must be personally safer, and you will get the money anyway. That way you've got everything on your side.'

'Yes, but they will have to close if enough of us say that,' replied Nicky. 'You know, I'm going to be happy there. I like looking after those old people, getting to know the different characters that they are, hearing about what they've done in their previous lives. And another thing is that I can tell that Stella doesn't want to close. I like her and I admire her character, and the other two nurses. They really look after those old people and care for them. They don't want to leave them, to send them somewhere else, just because they're scared of fighting the virus together. It's not a simple choice. Mum, what do you think?'

'I think it's up to you, Nicky,' said Yvonne. 'I don't think we should pressure you at all. It's your life and your decision. But you are only eighteen, you know, with all your life before you, and there are so many things you could do with your life.' She paused for some time. 'No. I'm not going to say one way or the other. This is for you. You decide and take responsibility for yourself.'

Nicky felt her mind was in a whirl, with so many considerations to bear in mind. They were all quiet again.

'Sleep on it tonight, Nicky,' said John. 'You've got all tomorrow to think about it, and you don't have to tell her until Monday.'

That's what she decided to do: think about it some more, and then still think about it overnight. Nicky cleared away the dirty plates and dishes and washed up in the kitchen vigorously and noisily.

Then an atmosphere of calm deliberation descended.

Nothing much was said on the Sunday morning. Nicky had her breakfast in silence, moved about, went for a walk on her own.

Then after lunch, everyone was sitting in the lounge, reading papers, Sean playing with his phone.

'OK, then,' Nicky suddenly burst out. 'I've made up my mind. I listened to you last night, and I've been thinking. I was awake a lot in the night. I have decided I'm going to move into Woodside Lodge until it's all over.' She paused. No-one said anything. They all looked at her. 'I agree with you that the best for me would be to stay at home here, not go in, take the money and wait. Then I would spend all the time thinking of the nurses and anyone else who goes in, getting on with caring for the old people, knowing the risks and going bravely on, fighting what comes and being proud of what they're doing. Not to go would be the easy thing, the selfish thing, and when it's all over, what will I think about myself? I'm young and I'm physically strong. I ought to have a good enough defence against the virus. So that's why I've made my mind up. I'm going to earn my pay, go and join Stella, stand with her looking after the old people, and we can fight whatever comes our way.'

Nicky looked round from one to the other. No-one spoke. She had been standing as she made her little bit of a speech. Her mother, Yvonne, got up out of her chair and came over to her. She took her in her arms and held her, as she did when she was a small girl, but had seldom done since. She hugged her and put her head on her shoulder.

'Oh, I'm so proud of you, Nicky, so proud.' And she continued to hold her in silence.

Eventually, her father said, 'Well, if that's what you want then, Nicky, good luck to you.'

'I hope you don't regret it,' said Sean, still looking into his phone.

Her mother clung to her for what seemed a long time. When she finally pulled her face away, Nicky felt that her shoulder was wet.

'Well done, Nicky.' Yvonne's red eyes looked into Nicky's face. 'You're doing one of the bravest things I've ever heard of. I'm so proud of you.'

Just after nine o' clock on Monday morning, Linda Doyle, who was not in that day because she had worked all weekend, telephoned Stella. She judged that by that time breakfasts would be over and Stella, who would have helped to serve it, would have gone back to her private lounge upstairs.

'Hello, Stella. I've been thinking about what you told us on Saturday. I was thinking about it all yesterday, and when I went home at two o' clock, I discussed it with my husband. Though I had told him about it on Saturday night, we didn't properly discuss it because he was glued to the television "Match of the Day", wondering what was going to happen to the last bit of the football season.

'But we decided, yesterday afternoon, that I couldn't keep coming in to work at the Lodge because I have to put my family first. The children are aged five and six and they are in the local infant school. Dave, my husband, would have to keep going to work, and I could have the usual childcare to take the children to school in the morning or to fetch them back home in the afternoon. They need me, though, to be with them, put them to bed, give them breakfast, with Dave as usual doing that if I'm on early shift. If you weren't isolating, I would keep coming into work each day, although even then, if it gets into the Lodge, I would run the risk of bringing it home here and giving it to all three of them, so, all things considered, I'll have to say "No". I'm very sorry, Stella, but there's one thing I'm not sure of and I don't know whether you can tell me. It's this thing about key workers. Would I count as a key worker? If so, my children could go to school full-time every day, and if I was in the Lodge all the time, Dave and the childcare person might be able to manage their breakfast , tea and putting them to bed, although we don't know how long this whole thing is going to last. What about "key worker", though?'

'That's what I'm not sure of, either, Linda, whether care home workers count as key workers. Personally, I doubt it, because the Government don't seem to bother about making much provision for us, anyway, and it would be better if the staff made their decisions on the assumption that we would not be key workers. I don't think many homes are going to do what I've decided to do, anyway. They'll just soldier on and see what happens, especially the ones owned by a network of larger companies. The small ones, including us, can be a law to themselves.' After a pause in which Linda didn't want to say anything else, she continued: 'Well, you've given me your decision, Linda, and that's absolutely fine. I quite understand your position, and from your point of view, I'm sure you are doing the right thing. Thank you for letting me know promptly, as I asked.

'So far, Laura and Kath have told me that they can't isolate with me, as they are in the same position as you, though Jo told me that she will do it if I go ahead. Thank you, Linda. I'm going to treat everyone absolutely fairly. You will be paid, eventually mostly with Government money, and I'll keep your job open for you. I don't know yet whether I will have enough staff to make this work, because I haven't heard yet from Sam, Maggie and Nicky, and it's doubtful whether I can do it without Sam and Maggie. I've only got Jo up to now. So, thank you again, Linda. It's fine. I understand.'

Stella turned round to go and get her own breakfast and to drink some good, strong coffee. At the moment, she felt pessimistic about how the day would end. Sam and Maggie lived on their own, but Nicky was so young that she would probably be drawn along with her family's opinion about the whole thing.

At two o' clock, Stella and Sam had both fed themselves with some left-over lunch in the dining room, had cleared away quickly, and Sam followed Stella up to the office early. She asked him if he would like to speak to her before the other two arrived, but he said he would rather wait and hear what they had to say.

Maggie and Nicky arrived together, exactly on time. They sat in easy chairs round in a circle, and of the three people facing Stella, Maggie was by far the most assertive – in a happy, cheerful way – and it was clearly best to ask her what she thought of her proposal first.

Maggie looked happy and relaxed. For the first time, Stella had a sense of what was coming. 'I want to stay here and join you in your isolation,' she said, and smiled. 'You know I live on my own, Stella, and let's face it, I'm well into my forties and past the marrying age. In any case, I'm rather too – erm – well built for men to be really interested in me. Believe it or not, from a selfish point of view, I want to stay here and join in. I must say, I don't want to go into details, but I haven't been treated with much kindness for a good deal of my life, and that's why I'm still on my own, but everyone here has been so good to me. I love you all and I just want to stay here.'

She looked round at the others in turn, and Stella noticed how the corners of her mouth worked nervously as she made her little speech. She was a bit embarrassed as well as nervous, but there was no equivocation: she said straight out that she wanted to stay. Stella felt a great sense of relief. Notwithstanding the expertise of those who had refused so far, she was most anxious about Maggie and Sam.

Sam was the next one she asked to say what he thought. To her surprise, and for some reason that she did not understand, Sam asked if he could listen to what Nicky thought first.

'Well, yes, I suppose so,' Stella said. She did not want to linger. 'Are you OK to tell us what you think now, Nicky?' she asked.

'Yes, and I have decided to do the same as Maggie,' Nicky said without hesitation, though she was surprised at the way Sam had deferred to her. 'I want to move in and stay here. Just as Maggie said, in the three weeks I've been here, I feel I've got to know everyone so well, and everyone is so kind and considerate. I've discussed it with my family, and I could do as they said, which is just to stay at home and take the money. It would be the safest thing, and I have all my life ahead of me. But that would be the easiest option, and the most selfish one. It would be because I would be scared of catching the virus, and we know that could be fatal. I think that when the coronavirus comes and maybe spreads all over the country, as it has done over much of the rest of the world, it will be such a serious event that many years from now, people will look back on it, and what happened in it, and what its consequences were, and they will remember how it was for them. Well, one day in the years ahead, I hope to get married and have children of my own, and when they say, "What were you doing when the Covid-19 was on, Mummy?" I could reply, "Oh, I stayed at home and took my pay and looked after myself, scared even to go to the shops", or I could say, "I stayed in the care home where I worked, with about twenty-five other people, and helped look after them so that they could survive it." I am going to say the second, because that's what I am going to do.'

Stella and Maggie looked at her with a broad smile. Stella said, 'Thank you, Nicky,' and Maggie said, 'Well done.'

Now, they all looked towards Sam, and Stella gave an open-handed gesture, which was an invitation to speak.

'I wanted to hear what other people said first,' he began, 'so that I could find out if other people saw it just as I did. I am young, though older than Nicky' – he smiled across at her – 'and I see things just as she described. I will not be in anything like the danger that the guests in Woodside Lodge will be in. Being a chef, my opportunities in the future are not confined to care homes. I could get all sorts of jobs in many different companies and places and I would be safe. When you're young, though, like Nicky and I are, you have a desire and a need to prove yourself. My Great-Grandad's generation fought in the second World War. They faced physical, mortal danger and they showed their bravery when they stood up and fought. But the world changes, and our challenges are different. Because we are in this age and in these circumstances, we also have to prove ourselves. The heroes nowadays are the care workers and the nurses and the doctors working twelve hours non-stop in an operating theatre. It is not a physical, blood-stained test that we have to face, but it is still a test, one of intelligence, carefulness, showing that you can look after others in a different way. And it is not easy. As Nicky said, the easy thing is to run away and look after yourself, but bravery nowadays consists of doing the right thing, having the courage to work hard and look after others, to understand, and to work together with your colleagues and be loyal. Well, I'm staying with you, Stella, and I'm really glad that Nicky and Maggie feel the same way.'

'Oh, thank you, Sam,' said Stella.

Nicky continued for a short time to look at Sam. He and Maggie were the people she had seen the least of her colleagues in and around the Lodge, and she hadn't got to know them very well. As she looked at Sam, she realised that if you met him out in the street or in any other circumstances, you would never think he was a chef. For one thing, he was slim, and though he was young, his hair had a grey appearance, a sort of wispy grey. He also had a small moustache and a short grey stubble on chin and jaw. This gave an older appearance and Nicky knew it was quite the fashion among young men these days. The hair on top of his head was also short, and drawn back in a rather untidy and unkempt way: it was apparently casual, but in fact carefully managed to give a very masculine appearance. It was, though, what was inside his head that mattered to Nicky. What a way to think of things for a young man like him. She was impressed.

'Well,' Stella resumed. 'Thank you all again. How things change quickly. An hour ago, I had had three of the staff say "No" today, and I was thinking that I wouldn't be able to manage it with only me and Jo. Now you've all said "Yes", I can suddenly see how, with me, Jo and you three, we can all make it work. Thank you.'

They stood up to go, Sam to go home and Nicky and Maggie to work. Suddenly and uncharacteristically, Stella stepped across to Sam, hugged him and kissed his right cheek. Nicky was next, a kiss on the side of her face and a long, strong embrace. Then she put her arms as far round Maggie as she could get them, kissed her cheek, and then put her face against Maggie's and held her tight for some time. Sam and Nicky looked at each other and smiled, a little embarrassed, but happy.

'Oh, I don't deserve you all,' said Stella as she broke away from Maggie. 'Thank you,' and she flopped down into her easy chair and watched them all troop out of the office, briefly smiling back at them. She felt the tears pricking the backs of her eyes, and leaned forward and put her head in her hands.

Chapter 7

When Stella had collected herself together, and had gone through into her private sitting room, her landline phone rang. It was Jo.

'Stella, I've had a sleep and just got up and switched the TV on. They're giving out announcements that the Prime Minister is going to broadcast to the nation at eight-thirty tonight.'

'Oh!' Stella expressed her exasperation. 'You don't say he's decided on lockdown. Thank heaven if he has. They obviously had made a decision to abandon so-called "herd immunity" at the Cobra last Monday.'

'Stella, I think it's worth sending round a message this afternoon. Most of the guests will be doing jigsaws on a Monday, so if we tell them about the broadcast and say that it will be on in the kitchen lounge at that time, and would they please watch it there or in their own rooms. Then we should all get the instructions before everyone except me goes to bed tonight.'

'Yes,' replied Stella. 'Well, if that's what we're told, we've beaten him to it, Jo. The good news is that just now, Maggie, Sam and Nicky said they have decided to move in and see this thing through with you and me. The other three, Kath, Linda and Laura, said "No", all of them because they have children and have to put their families first. I told them it was quite understandable and that I didn't mind. I didn't think we'd be able to do it without Maggie and Sam, but just now, at two o' clock, they both said that they would stay with us, and Nicky too, and I was so overjoyed I kissed them all. Isn't it good?'

'It certainly is. I must say that I had my doubts about whether enough of them would be willing to move in, but there we are, Stella. You've got a mighty good staff.'

'OK, Jo. Thank you. Well, if we could talk a bit tonight when you come for night-shift, we'll start getting everything organised ready for tomorrow.'

'Yes. See you, then, Stella.'

'See you later. Thank you.'

After that, Stella rang Kath, Laura and Linda to confirm with them that they were not to come into the Lodge from tomorrow onwards.

With that, Stella went back into the office and down the central staircase into the laundry lounge. Nicky was in there, and so she heard Stella apologise for interrupting the jigsaws, to ask everyone if they would please make sure that they were in the kitchen lounge to watch a Prime Ministerial broadcast at eight-thirty that evening. Other than that, she said, would they please watch it in their rooms because she thought it would be important and that everyone would have to know what he said. Stella made a mental note of everyone who was not there and, after asking Nicky to go round all the rooms and to give that same message to everyone who had stayed in them, she went through into the laundry to tell Maggie. Maggie seemed really pleased and excited, promising that she would be watching. Stella returned to her room upstairs, intending to wait until she thought Sam had arrived home, before telephoning him with the same news.

Jo arrived to start the night shift half an hour earlier that evening, so that she could watch the broadcast with Stella in her room, and they could discuss the implications of it immediately it had finished.

'Yes. That's what I thought he would say and now we've all heard it,' began Stella after the broadcast was over. 'This, at last, is lockdown and the "herd immunity" nonsense is just history. They are suppressing the virus with all they've got. They were frightened rigid by that broadcast on 5th March of a possible 250,000 deaths. They've waited all through February and March, watching the Italians bringing the virus by 'plane into Britain, and now that every other European country except Sweden has closed its borders and locked down, they have come to their senses and we are doing it. Of course, we are now four weeks behind Italy and two weeks behind Spain, because we waited for the Cheltenham Festival and various football matches to finish. Still, despite lockdown, they lifted airport restrictions on 17th March, nearly a week ago.

'Anyway, Jo, let's check with each other what he's just said that we can and can't do.'

'Staying at home was the very first thing he said,' began Jo, 'and you can't meet friends or relatives who don't live with you. Everyone is allowed to go out to buy food and medicine, to take one form of exercise each day and to get medical attention.'

'Yes,' agreed Stella. 'Those are the main things, but that about travelling to and from work won't apply to us because we are going to do our own local lockdown. Because all the residents except the staff are clearly elderly, that makes them the most vulnerable kind of people, and we can't have people going in and out because that is what will cause transmission. I don't think the social distancing of two metres apart can apply to us, either, because, as we are all living in one building with no-one visiting, and no-one going in or out except into the garden, we must count as one large family, and we can't avoid breathing each other's air at some time. Do you agree?'

'Yes, certainly, but I think there is a need for face masks when staff are in close personal contact with guests, especially with getting up, showering, or having medication in the morning. We must never forget that we have four guests with diabetes and three with asthma, and I think those two conditions make people the most vulnerable to this virus if infection occurs.'

'Absolutely, Jo. I agree. So no distancing, but masks always worn by staff when in close personal contact with guests. The constant watch by staff for symptoms will obviously have to continue, and they will be what we have already told them: a high temperature, a cough and any trouble with breathing. It's not officially listed as a symptom yet, but I'm increasingly sure it will be, and so if anyone complains that they can't smell or taste, we can take it seriously, Jo, and I'll tell Nicky and Maggie that as well. I think you and I should check oxygen levels of any suspects every day, and take blood pressure when necessary.'

'Yes, well I think that covers everything he said, Stella, and a bit more. It doesn't seem much of a list, really, but I think the simpler you keep things, the better they will be remembered. We wrote a list of the symptoms, and I think we'd better type out a longer list now.'

'I'll do that when you're on your rounds tonight, Jo, and I'll also make it clear that everyone can use our garden and grounds for exercise.

'Then we'll have to plan what the living arrangements are going to be for this period of lockdown. Would you like to come and live with me in my own private quarters here, Jo? As you know, I have my own bedroom and sitting room, bathroom, toilet and kitchen. Well, I have two single beds in my bedroom, and obviously I only use one of them, so we could move the other into the sitting room, here, and that gives us each a private bedroom. We can share the kitchen, bathroom and toilet, and the sitting room can have a double function.'

'Well, that's very kind of you, Stella. Thank you. Considering that there are five of us, it would be most convenient having both of us stowed away up here, and it saves me bringing any furniture in.'

'Yes. I'll have to speak to Maggie, Sam and Nicky as soon as they get here in the morning. I hope they'll have some kind of portable sleeping equipment they can bring in and use. We have the two rooms for intermediates vacant at the moment, but I don't want to block those yet, because when they are needed, I think it will be with no notice at all. There's no reason why all three of them, Maggie, Nicky and Sam, shouldn't use the family bathroom and toilet that goes with those rooms, though. They already use the toilet facilities because it's the only staff toilet we have apart from mine – which will be ours.'

'Oh, yes,' agreed Jo. 'We'll have to see what they can bring in. By the way, you said as soon as Nicky comes in. Well, she's on afternoon tomorrow, but is she on afternoons after that? How's it going to be from then on?'

'I think the only thing is that if Nicky and I always do all the mornings, six to two – that makes two of us for breakfasts – and if you could do the medication round, that makes three. If Maggie helps with lunch, that will be three doing lunch, with me as well. Sam, of course, stays with what he always does, breakfast and lunch and an evening snack with soup. Maggie could be on afternoons every day to deal with laundry, but could begin early to help with lunch, and finish early, immediately after supper. I think Sam will have to do without his relief once a month. We'll have to see how long all this lasts.'

'Oh, yes. I can see how that can all work out,' said Jo. 'So that means me on nights all the time, then?'

'For this week, yes,' said Stella, 'but you and I can swap nights for the morning shift whenever it's convenient. Of course, there can be absolutely no visitors from now on, and the entertainment on Wednesday and Friday afternoons will be cancelled, and no outings on Tuesdays. Jigsaws and board games carry on. I'll have to tell Sam to order all food online, and even then, it's quarantined before use. If there are things he can't get online, I'll fetch them in our minibus and then we'll wash them down and quarantine them.'

'Yes: just a bit of sorting out of sleeping accommodation tomorrow, then.'

'Right. The only thing is, this is for seven days a week, so we'll have to see how long it lasts. Anyway, we're not going anywhere at the weekends; there'll be nowhere to go. The Prime Minister says so.' They ended in smiles.

Early the next day, Tuesday, the three other staff agreed to the new shift arrangements, as it was much the same for Sam and Maggie, and they also agreed immediately to using each of the lounges as their living area, and to use the family bathroom upstairs.

Nicky said sleeping would be no problem for her, because at home her family had a spare, portable foam bed that lies directly onto the floor, but is thick and comfortable and she has used it many times. It just folds and stands on its end in a corner of the room when not in use. She said it needed bed linen, but she could bring that in when her dad brought the bed in the car. She said she would be happy to keep it in the corner of the laundry lounge. Sam , for his part, also had in his flat a folding camp bed which he used for visiting his family in London, where accommodation was limited. He said he could fold it and store it in a corner of the dining room, and that could be his bedroom. The only one with any problem was Maggie, who lived on her own but possessed only one single bed, a normal, permanent bed. She agreed with Stella that if it was brought to the Lodge, it could be stored on its end in a corner of the kitchen lounge. Then, for the time being, she could sleep in one of the rooms for intermediates, on the understanding that, if an intermediate moved in, Maggie would vacate her sleeping room and move down to the kitchen lounge to sleep on her own bed, which could easily be up-ended and stand in a corner of the kitchen lounge each day.

Tuesday morning at breakfast, after Jo had done the medication round, and as Nicky was serving breakfast, Stella, very loudly, asked everyone to wait in the kitchen lounge, next door, before they went back to their rooms, so that she could tell them of the new arrangements in place after the Prime Minister's broadcast the night before.

'There'll still be the smell of breakfast in there. Couldn't we go into the laundry lounge, Stella?' asked Nicky quietly.

Stella winked at her, smiled, and said even more quietly, 'By the time they get to the laundry lounge, some of them will have forgotten what I asked. Ella will have done, although I notice Barbara is with her. I also notice Sid and Dennis are not here, though I think they often come late. Dennis sometimes forgets breakfast altogether. Anyway, I'll go to their rooms and tell them separately if they don't appear here at all.'

Nicky returned the smile and got on with serving the pots of tea, as they had had toast and it was getting towards the end of the meal. Point taken, Nicky thought. Soon after breakfast, therefore, everyone knew about the new arrangements, and accepted it all very quietly. Sid and Dennis arrived late, and were still chewing toast as Stella spoke. There were a few mutterings.

'I'll miss Kath,' said Margery. 'Who's going to give me my morning pill?'

'Jo or me.'

'I'm going into the garden with Sid,' called Chris. 'He can take me to parts of the garden that I've never seen.'

'Well, you be careful where you're going in that garden with Lorna,' called Maurice. No answer.

After that, everything seemed quietly normal, as Nicky and Stella went round the rooms attending to people. The day's outing had been cancelled, and there would be no more outings now. Stella made a list of the daily newspapers people said they wanted to read, because now they would all have to be delivered and there would be no more walks down to the local newsagent. Then, Stella had to drive down to the newsagent's in Chignall wearing her mask, explain to them what the situation was and give them a copy of the list. They were delighted. Sam, as usual, had all the afternoons off. He had a licence that enabled him to drive the minibus, and so he drove it back to his flat, picked up all the possessions and two sets of bed-linen he would need during the lockdown, loaded up his camp bed and took them all back to the Lodge.

Having previously warned them by telephone, Nicky then went with Sam back to her family's house, gathered up all the things she would need including two lots of bed-linen, and then loaded the foam bed into the minibus. Five minutes later, she and Sam unloaded everything into the Lodge.

By the end of the afternoon, Maggie had finished with the day's laundry. Sam took her to her flat and, though it was difficult, the two of them managed to balance her single bed across the tops of the seats in the bus and that, together with all her personal equipment, was soon on its end in the corner of the kitchen lounge, for use when it would ultimately be needed. Meanwhile, Stella and Jo between them had managed to push Stella's spare single bed through into the sitting-room for Jo's use during the duration of the new stage of living they had all embarked upon.

Sam made and served the soup that evening, Stella helping him, as that was usually her job, and after clearing up, it was a quiet evening after a tiring day. Nicky and Maggie joined Sam in watching TV in the kitchen lounge before occupying their new sleeping quarters.

Wednesday morning passed as if the routine had always been arranged that way. Everyone was either busy in their rooms or sitting in the lounges reading newspapers, all delivered that morning for the first time. Julia Nash's "Music and Movement" session after lunch had been cancelled and, as the guests had not been warmed up for it, Stella decided it was best not to start the "House-party-type games", as Linda called them, in the afternoon. It was very pleasant weather, and, at Stella's subtle suggestions, many guests decided to get some fresh air in the garden.

A group of three or four people had gathered round Sid as he walked round the boundary of the garden, acknowledging his expertise if they wanted to examine closely any of the flowers, shrubs or small trees in that area. Nicky went across and joined them. At the far edge of the garden were many bushes and trees which were the beginning of the wood after which the Lodge had originally been named. Although there was still another week in March, some of the bushes were covered in a lovely white blossom that appeared snowy from a distance. 'Are they hawthorn, Sid?' Jane asked.

'No. Hawthorn has white flowers, like that, but they don't come out till the summer, the end of April or beginning of May time. Those are the blackthorn, and the fruit are called sloes. That is always the first blossom to come out in the hedgerow in Spring. They are not usually out at this time, but we've had a mild, wet winter, so everything will be a bit early. It looks as if the Spring will be dry, though.'

'Sloes can be made into wine, can't they, Sid?' Jane continued.

'It's sometimes called sloe gin,' said Martin. 'My mother used to make some each year.'

'Those trees further along have also got some blossom coming,' added Jane, wanting to take an interest in the surroundings.

'That really proves my point,' said Sid. 'They are cherry trees, and they are the first trees to blossom, but not until April, and they are at least two weeks early.'

'We could lean over and pick the cherries and eat them, couldn't we?' Martin really wanted to join in the conversation.

'You wouldn't want to eat them,' said Sid, with a laugh. 'They're bird cherry, and the actual cherries are black and really bitter. The fruit does come fairly early, and I suppose the tree's called bird cherry because the birds do eat them, but I expect they go straight through them pretty quickly.'

'And they have plopped the stones on the ground so that they have spread along the ground this side.'

'Exactly. Thank you, Martin,' said Sid with some impatience, which was unusual for him. 'You can tell if the stones are from bird cherry because they are all wrinkly. We must be near the southern edge of their range because bird cherry trees don't grow any further south than Leicestershire. You can see that they are about average height for a small tree, about twenty feet, but the best cherry trees for eating the fruit are called the Gean, and they are tall and slender, and grow to eighty or ninety feet high.'

The little group turned from the far boundary of the garden, and after they had taken a few steps back towards the Lodge, they came across the clump of snowdrops that Linda and Nicky had seen two or three weeks ago, when Sid had been kneeling down looking at them and saying that he admired them. There were one or two tiny blooms left, but most of the snowdrops were now falling back in the face of the advancing Spring.

'The snowdrops are well past the best,' moaned Sid, 'now that they've led everybody out of the winter.' Then, looking across to his left, he continued, 'Here, here, everyone will know what these are.'

'I wandered lonely as a cloud,' began Jane.

'Oh leave that off,' called Martin. 'Come down from the cloud, down to earth. They're daffodils, Sid.'

'Right,' answered Sid. 'They're the strongest and the first, apart from the snowdrops, of course. Then we'll have the crocuses further over, the elegance of the tulips, the polyanthus and the narcissi.' The others acknowledged Sid's expertise and leadership by now walking along in silence, admiring everything about them.

Suddenly, they heard a small bird singing. 'What's that, then? Who is he, the first summer visitor to this country?' asked Sid, but there was no immediate reply. Unusually with small birds, they could see him as well as hear him, towards the top of one of the small beech trees, busily pecking into small buds on the tiny twigs, a small, delicate bird with an olive-brown back, singing as he moved along, sweet notes alternating up and down, very distinctly.

'Chiffchaff,' said a new voice to the group. Nicky's face relaxed into a smile as she turned and saw Sam.

'I thought you were still in the kitchen lounge, Sam,' she said. 'I saw you talking with Maggie in there.'

'Yes. I was trying to persuade her to come out here. In the end, she wouldn't, but I could see this little group wandering about over here, so I thought I'd come and join you.'

They all walked in silence, slowly, happily, enjoying the Spring air. Finally, they started to drift back to the Lodge. Probably looking forward to a cup of tea, thought Nicky. Stella said she'd do it this afternoon, so I think I'll let her.

'Were your family OK about you staying here?' asked Sam.

'Well, Sean, my brother, said he thought I was a bit silly, and should look after myself, but Mum and Dad just said it was my decision, and left me to it. But when I thought about it, there was no question: I was convinced I should stay here and fight this thing.'

'Me, too,' said Sam. 'I don't run away from things. I just stand up for myself – and other people.'

With that, they followed the others in for tea.

Sam served the soup for supper that Wednesday evening. He told Stella he would always do that in the evenings from now on. He might as well, he had said, now that he was living on the premises all the time, and he could still prepare something to eat cold at some time in the morning, as he always had done. After the tomato soup, he distributed to the guests as well as Nicky, Maggie, Jo and Stella, the sardine tart with salad dressing, which was his offering for that day. He had also prepared two small pasta salads for Lorna and Barbara, in consideration of their fish allergies. Now that there were five staff eating together at that time of day, all the soup plates, dishes and cups and saucers were whisked away into the kitchen, washed, cleared and stored away in no time.

Every evening after that, all the guests went away to their own rooms from about eight o' clock, and if they wanted to watch any TV, they watched it there on their own sets. Strolls in the garden were popular in the summer, but the evenings were too dark and chilly for that yet.

The staff, though, had no base except where they were going to sleep, and Maggie, Stella and Jo tended to gather in Stella's sitting room albeit with Jo's bed in there, as all three of them were sleeping upstairs. Sam and Nicky sat in the kitchen lounge, as Sam was sleeping in the dining room and Nicky in the laundry lounge. Sam made them each a milky drink later in the kitchen and brought it through. He didn't offer the same for the ladies upstairs, because they had Stella's own private kitchen.

In the kitchen lounge there were two two-seater settees, suitably upholstered in an upright position for the elderly guests, and when Nicky and Sam settled in the evening for some late TV watching, they sat together in one of them because it was suitably positioned for viewing. Nicky realised immediately the implications of their sitting together, but it rather amused her, and the three senior staff were in the sitting room upstairs. But, she reflected, he seemed a very pleasant young man who had always been courteous to her, and she had been very impressed by what he had said to Stella at the two o' clock meeting in the office on Monday. The novelty of adjusting to the new arrangements and the fact that her working day had started at 6 am, made Nicky feel rather tired.

When they had been sitting and watching for about twenty minutes, though, the inevitable happened. Sam moved very slightly closer, and took Nicky's hand very gently in his. Nicky, just as gently, withdrew her hand.

'Right, well, I think I'd better explain things to you, Sam,' said Nicky, as Sam turned sharply to look at her. 'It's obvious that we are two young people living in the same building, for we don't know how long, and that we both have our sleeping arrangements on the ground floor. It is also obvious that you are a very nice young man who behaves towards me in a friendly and courteous manner, and I hope I do the same towards you. But none of that means that I want a physical relationship with you. I do know how to look after myself, you know. When I worked at Debenham's for two years, there was a young man in the office who came on forcefully in one of the corridors during the Christmas party. I really had to wrestle with him. I forced him away and kicked him where it hurt. I didn't see him for the rest of the evening, or ever again. As for a physical relationship, I did all that with a lad in my form at school when I was sixteen. If I do any of that sort of thing again, it will only be with someone I have known for a long time, that I have a lot in common with, and that I really love. You don't qualify on any of those counts, Sam. I've had plenty of other boyfriends, though, and I like being friendly and sociable with boys, but that's as far as it goes. So you, Sam, can hold my hand,' – and here she very gently and deliberately put her hand back in Sam's – 'and we can kiss if you like, and be friends together, but that's all. No more.'

All this had been spoken quietly and in a low tone, and very firmly. Sam was taken aback at how composed and mature she was. She was not nervous at all. Sam was also quite relieved now, as he sat there holding Nicky's hand after she had said all that, and he knew where he stood.

'Oh, you've been around a bit, then,' he said, just for the sake of saying something that didn't mean anything.

'Let me tell you something about me, about my character.' Nicky had obviously not finished yet, and wanted to add something else. 'I said I liked being sociable and friendly, and that is true, and it is on the surface, but just a bit underneath, where you think about serious things, I am rock solid. I look after myself and I know what I want and don't want.' Sam nodded. 'I get it from my Dad if you want to know. He works as a salesman during the autumn and winter, but it's seasonal, September to February. From February through the summer, he works happily in the office at Anscombe's, but also part-time, sometimes nights and weekends, he has a gut-wrenching job with an undertaker. I'm not telling you any details, but he's told me some of the things he's had to do, and I can tell you, he's made of mighty stern stuff underneath his happy and friendly exterior.'

'Oh, right.' Sam pulled his hand back again. He still didn't really know what to say. 'I think I'll go and make two milky Ovaltines, if you want one.'

'Yes. Thank you.' Nicky was smiling, still calm, composed and happy.

Sam was happy, too, as he made the drinks in the kitchen. He had switched off the TV at the beginning of their conversation. He left his own drink in the kitchen and took Nicky's to her where she was still sitting in the lounge.

'Thanks, Sam,' she said. 'See you in the morning. Goodnight.' She stood up and took her drink through to her foam bed in the laundry lounge.

'Goodnight,' said Sam, and went back to the kitchen.

There were the usual board games in full swing on Thursday afternoon in the laundry lounge. It was four o' clock and Stella had collected the cups after tea and was going through the kitchen lounge to take them for washing up, when she saw Marsha and May standing at the large window in the kitchen lounge. Outside the Lodge, the path leading from the road to the front door was for pedestrians. The drive into the building went past the laundry lounge window and round to the door at the end of the laundry for deliveries, and a bit further on to the outside corridor door for doctors, medical visitors and ambulances, and then further round for the small car park. Woodside Avenue had a gentle bend as cars approached the Lodge past the kitchen lounge window on the other side. It was at this window that Marsha and May were standing, waving excitedly. Then Stella could see that two cars had stopped on the road and a family had got out of each and stood on the pavement waving in at the ladies and blowing kisses.

Obviously, this was the new style of visiting, and, being unable to come inside, this was the next best thing they could do. The families, especially the young grandchildren, were desperate to see their grandmothers, jumping, moving along, waving, brandishing things that looked like birthday presents. Stella swallowed, held back the tears, and went on and into the kitchen. As it was late in the day, the traffic was heavy and Stella made a mental note of the small queue of traffic that formed. She made another mental note to ask guests to tell their relatives on the phone that they were welcome to come into the car park for their through-window visiting. Within a few days, more cars began to occupy the car park than usual, and the remote visiting took place through the lounge window on each side of the building.

Chapter 8

Another two weeks had passed. Everyone inside Woodside Lodge had adjusted to the new "internal" way of living, accepted the new routines without much comment, and just got on with day-to-day living. The "external" visiting, looking through the window, increased and was similarly accepted as part of the daily routine. Sam and Nicky continued their friendship, smiling as they passed each other, talking quietly, and occasionally they held hands as they watched the late TV in the kitchen lounge. Sometimes, Maggie sat with them, but mostly she stayed upstairs.

A few incidents occurred on the national scene. On the evening of Friday 27th March, the Prime Minister was admitted to St Thomas's hospital in London and tested positive for the virus. A routine was started, prompted by announcements on the media, for citizens to come out and stand at the front of their houses or flats and clap to show gratitude for the NHS and the emergency services. Some of the guests at Woodside Lodge went out and stood clapping on the front lawn for two or three minutes. Lew took a stainless-steel saucepan from the kitchen and banged it with a metal spoon. The staff did not go out because they thought it would appear that they were accepting the applause, but stated that they were not NHS staff and were not treated as if they were emergency services. The first day for this was Thursday 2nd April, and on that day, the Prime Minister was moved into intensive care at St Thomas's. Jo and Stella exchanged glances as they heard this news.

'My word, that must be serious,' said Jo, and Stella nodded.

'It seems he's not on a ventilator, but having special oxygen treatment. That's good,' Stella said.

The media began announcing the daily numbers of deaths from Covid-19, and on Wednesday 8th April it was 950 deaths for that day. Jo's comment was that that meant that all those people must have been infected with the virus on or before 25th of March.

On the afternoon of 9th April, the laundry lounge was quite full with guests playing various board games, but Nicky noticed that Martin wasn't there. That was unusual, because Nicky knew that he was a great fan of scrabble, and usually played it right through the afternoon with Vic and Mick, who spent a lot of the time not only playing but also arguing about some Test match series that had taken place about ten years ago when Australia were the visitors. Sometimes the argument might have been about an FA Cup final which occurred even further ago than that. Today, though, they had not started a game because Martin had not come through to play.

Nicky went to Martin's room and found him sitting back in his easy chair. He was not reading a newspaper, or doing anything except sitting with a rather distant look on his face. He told Nicky to tell Vic and Mick that he wasn't coming because he felt a bit tired.

Nicky relayed the message. 'H'm. Worn out with all that sitting and reading this morning,' commented Vic, and they got on with their first game. Later, Stella took the teas to the board game players, while Nicky looked into any occupied rooms to see if anyone needed any tea bringing. Martin was keen to accept one. He told Nicky that he didn't feel too well. He thought he had a touch of indigestion after his lunch, and the tea was just what he wanted.

Stella had gone early into the dining room to set out the supper. Nicky had also set out some cutlery, but had then gone to check that the board games had all been put away tidily. She began to have a nagging unease about Martin's tiredness, and she hadn't seen him come through to supper yet, so she went to check in No. 4.

A few seconds later, she came running, white-faced, full pelt back through the lounge, across the hall in one stride, through the kitchen lounge and then bolted straight for the door to the dining room. Immediately she opened it, she could see who she wanted.

'Stella!' she blurted out, but then couldn't think what else to say, because she didn't want to alarm the guests. Therefore, she just beckoned, quickly, sharply, with tension. The look on her face, and the quick, nervous action told Stella all she needed to know. She put down what she had been carrying onto the nearest table, and went across the dining room in one quick, gliding movement. Nicky had backed into the kitchen lounge, and, as she came through, Stella closed the door behind her.

'It's Martin,' blurted out Nicky in a hoarse, rasping whisper. 'I went to see if he was coming into the dining room, but he was lying on the bed and I called to him but I couldn't rouse him, and he seemed so still. So I walked over to him and I touched his hand as it was lying there beside him and it was cold.' Once what she had to say had come tumbling out, Nicky felt faint and went limp.

Because she was standing opposite her, Stella was able to catch hold of Nicky, and she guided her to a chair close by and let her subside into it.

'I'll go and see to him,' said Stella, and she set off briskly to the hallway door. She might have run, but when Nicky said Martin was cold, she had a sense that she might be too late to help him.

Nicky, for her part, though she had initially wilted, collected herself immediately and rushed off after Stella. As they went across the laundry lounge, through the laundry and round into the corridor, they were caught by another flying figure. One of the guests in the dining room had gasped out a sense of urgency to Jo as she entered the dining room, and she had reacted like a flash and set off.

Stella pushed open the door, burst in and went straight across to the bed. The sense of quiet and stillness was almost palpable. She leant across Martin as he lay there motionless, staring up at the ceiling. She brushed her hand lightly across the back of his hand. Then she touched his face, very lightly, just a quick stroke in passing. Next, her hands covered his eyes and closed the lids. She felt along his jaw, slowly, and then along the side of his neck, and looked back at Jo, close behind her: 'No pulse. Ring 999, Jo, on there.'' She pointed at the direct-line phone. She checked on the inside of the wrist, and then, as he was lying squarely on his back and had only a shirt on, she lay the side of her face heavily on his rib cage. After a long five seconds, she looked back at Jo on the phone: 'No. Nothing.' She snatched a small mirror from the top of the bedside cabinet and held it across his mouth, which was partly open, making sure to get close to his nostrils. Then she looked intently at the mirror, shook her head, and closed the mouth firmly.

Stella asked Nicky when she had last seen him. 'Cup-of-tea time, over two hours ago,' she said, weakly. Stella and Jo looked into each other's faces.

'It's been too long,' said Jo. 'Look at the colour.' Martin's complexion was like a smooth paste, the colour of vanilla. It had not begun to change colour yet, and his neck did not yet feel stiff, but the skin was very cool.

Jo, who had finished telephoning, turned back to Martin. 'I'll try,' she said, and pressed down on his chest on her crossed hands , one on top of the other, and let her weight rock down and back up and kept it going for thirty presses without response. While Jo did that, Stella went back to the mouth and prised it open again. He had a plate of false teeth across his upper jaw. With her index finger, Stella deftly hooked them out and put them on the top of the cabinet. She then felt around the inside of the mouth and the top of the throat. Jo stopped pumping the chest, and Stella closed his mouth.

'No. I'm sorry, Jo. I should have said before. There is a DNAR in place for Martin because of his weak heart, and I'm afraid this really is the end. We have tried our best beyond all reasonable doubt.' She turned to Nicky. 'You couldn't have done anything for him, Nicky,' she said. 'I'll go and ring Dr Attwood immediately. He can't do anything for him, but he's got to say he's dead before we can get Jim Borrett to come and take him away to the morgue. He may sign a certificate because he does know about him and we had two telephone consultations last week. I've been monitoring his blood pressure every day and it's way too low.'

She looked with some compassion at Nicky. 'You see, Nicky, we can provide medication for high blood pressure, but there's precious little we can do about low blood pressure. It is all consistent with what you said – the tiredness, the weakness, the feeling unwell, the vacant stare. I'm sorry, Nicky, but this is part of the job. Jo, could you just sit with her through in the laundry lounge while I make the phone call, and then I'll come and talk with her while we wait for the doctor.'

Stella came back quickly, having made the call. 'Dr Attwood says he is free, and will come now,' she said. 'You go and get your snack, Jo, and ask Sam to put ours aside until later.' Stella waited for Jo to go, and then resumed talking to Nicky. 'This may be a bit rough for you, Nicky, if it's your first time for dealing with something like this, and there's something else I need to tell you as well. I know you sleep in here. There's your foam bed standing up in the corner, and I don't know if you have realised this yet, but when a doctor or an ambulance comes when I've called them, they come round this side of the Lodge, past this side window, and round past the laundry door to the door at the beginning of the corridor. They all just get to know that, if they've been more than once. I'm telling you because they'll be coming round tonight after Dr Attwood's been. I expect Jim Borrett himself will come if it's late.' Stella stopped speaking momentarily because Nicky covered her face with her hands. 'What's the matter?'

'It may be my Dad as well,' said Nicky. 'He works for Borrett's part-time and sometimes gets called out at night.'

Stella was quiet, and then said: 'As I say, it's part of the job and you'll get used to it, but I suppose it may be worse if you see your Dad.' She paused. 'Sorry, Nicky.'

They sat together for a few minutes, silently. Then Stella stirred. 'You sit here for as long as you like, Nicky. Go through into the dining room and kitchen when you feel like eating and drinking. Don't say anything to the other guests if you meet any. If they ask, tell them that the doctor's coming. They'll know what's happened in the morning. News of these things is always better in the morning rather than at night. I've got to go and clear the room now and clean it while I'm waiting for Dr Attwood. I'll have to leave Martin as he is until the doctor's seen him, but I'll make a start by collecting his personal possessions and the rest of his clothes together. His wife has died, but he has a son and daughter-in-law living some distance away and I'll have to phone them immediately the doctor's been.'

'Oh, he couldn't even see them before the end,' said Nicky.

Stella shook her head. 'Even if we could have contacted them in time, we would not have allowed them in. If you're isolating, Nicky, and especially if you're isolating a whole building containing many people, you have got to be absolutely rigid in enforcing it. Otherwise, there's no point in doing it at all.'

'Yes, Stella.' These two short words carried a whole welter of understanding and feeling.

'Will your Dad be upset if he comes here and sees you?'

'No. He really loves me and feels for me, but he's as tough as old boots underneath. He didn't try to persuade me not to isolate here, because he knows I'm the same as he is.' Stella looked at her and thought she would make a fine nurse one day. 'I'll go now,' she said. 'See you later.'

As soon as she had gone, Dr Attwood came briskly through the door and strode straight to the head of the bed. He touched Martin's hands, face, jaw, neck and wrist. He shook his head. 'As your tone implied on the phone, it's too late and he is dead. He has gone too far to revive him.'

'There's a DNAR,' said Stella, 'and you know about the low blood pressure.' The doctor nodded.

Then the paramedics came in, complete with defibrillator. They looked at the doctor. He waved them away: 'Too late.' They retreated quickly, quietly.

Later, after Nicky had had something to eat and two warm drinks, she decided she didn't want to watch any TV that evening with Sam, and went back into the laundry lounge and read for a while. Then she decided to switch off the lights and sit for a while to be alone with her thoughts. She drew one half of the curtains back so that some street light from Woodside Avenue gave a little glow for her to see the furniture by. A feeling of peace and calm enveloped her.

Just when she was thinking of going to bed, she heard other, muffled movements. She saw the dark Transit van move slowly down the side drive and even in the gloaming she saw the name "James Borrett – Private ambulance" in small, discreet letters on the bottom of the door.

She got up and walked quietly through the laundry and into the corridor containing the outside door. The lighting was low and the two men who came in with their stretcher were no more than silhouettes, but Nicky recognised her Dad's profile. Noiselessly, they moved along to No. 4, where Stella ushered them inside. They re-emerged fairly quickly and Nicky kept her distance, leaning on the wall in the semi-darkness. She noticed, though, that her Dad looked up momentarily. He had to attend carefully to what he was doing, and could not look or nod or speak, but Nicky knew he would have noticed her. So did Stella, who walked along with them until they were outside, and then closed the door.

Nicky went back to sit for another short time in the dark before going to bed. She was not surprised to hear the door handle turn softly, and knew it would be Stella who came in and sat in one of the easy chairs. 'Well done, Nicky,' she said. 'I'll just sit for a moment if you don't mind. I've told Jo I'll do the night shift tonight. I've got some things to sort out in my mind and I've got some planning to do in the office.'

'Will there be someone new in No. 4 in a day or two?' asked Nicky.

'It's usually a few days before that happens,' said Stella. 'We'll have to do what we call a deep clean and then there's all the fresh laundry to go in. Dr Attwood decided that he could sign a certificate which he has done, so I can give it to Martin's son when it has been quarantined with everything else that was Martin's. The doctor said he could sign it because there have been two consultations with Martin recently, and it was absolutely clear that it had nothing to do with the virus. If he hadn't signed it, the coroner would have ordered a post-mortem, which would have caused some delay.

'After the deep clean, I'll advertise in the local press and in the "Senior Citizen", a news-sheet that one of the insurance companies specialising in elderly customers sends out to a targeted number of people. There's a leaflet delivery service that covers Chignall and Gainsford as well, so I might send flyers out with them. But I don't think I'll get any response. The elderly people and their relatives will want to use the visiting carer companies for as long as they can rather than residential homes. The carers are scrupulous in wearing masks and gloves and screens and using sanitisers everywhere they go. If they can afford it, there are also live-in carers around this area, though they are the most expensive of all. If

I don't get any response, I'll just leave it empty. I am sure, though, that although Brookfields Hospital has not pre-booked us, we will get intermediates pretty soon now.'

'Quite an industry, isn't it?' said Nicky.

'An increasing amount of custom,' replied Stella.

The news spread quickly at breakfast on Friday 10th April and, as usual, conversation was reduced to a murmur. There was, as always, the quietness and sober reflection as people went about their daily routines. On that day, it was also announced that the Prime Minister had been moved out of intensive care and back into an ordinary Covid-19 ward.

Then, on Thursday 16th April, the lockdown was extended for another three weeks. There had also been another 800 people who had died of Covid-19 on that day alone. By 23rd April it was announced that in the UK a total of 18,500 people had died of Covid-19, and that figure included the 2,000 people who had died in care homes.

Martin's son came four days later to collect clothes, belongings, spare cash and various documents, including the certificate of which Jim Borrett said he would need a copy. The funeral was set for Tuesday 28th April, but Martin's son said that the crematorium in Gainsford would allow only seven socially-distanced people to attend the service, and there were more than seven relatives. Therefore, the family had arranged a "drive by" funeral, and these were becoming common. This was because Martin had been a well-known local politician, and many people would want to show their respects by lining the route as the hearse passed by.

The family had told Stella the date, time and route of the procession to the crematorium and therefore, on the 28th April, nearly all the guests at Woodside Lodge, and Stella, Jo, Nicky, Maggie and Sam stood on the front lawn of the Lodge at precisely 11.10 am and watched Martin pass by on his final journey. Some bowed their heads as he passed by; others bowed more fully; others stood and looked respectfully and their minds were full of sorrow and memories. There were a few handkerchiefs in evidence and nearly everyone was red-eyed.

On that day, it was announced that the total number of deaths from Covid-19 in the UK was now 27,500, which made the UK the third highest total of all the countries in the world. Only the USA and Italy had had more deaths.

Stella mentioned to Jo, Maggie, Sam and Nicky, as they met at 2 pm that same day, that, now that the entertainers on Wednesday and Friday afternoons had been cancelled, it would be good if they could think of something to raise the spirits of the guests. She said the media people on TV seemed to want to make a big thing of this year's VE day because it marked 75 years since Victory in Europe actually took place in 1945. There were even three or four of the guests who could remember it, and Stella knew of a trumpet-player in Chignall who usually played the "Last Post" on Remembrance Sunday in the Church. She thought she could persuade him to play that in Woodside Avenue outside the Lodge at 11am, and if they all gathered, reasonably distanced although in theory they were one family, they could observe the two minutes' silence.

The authorities had postponed the Bank holiday, which would have been the Friday of the week they were in, May 1st, to the following Friday, as VE day was 8th May. If they could get the trumpeter to play outside in the morning, in the afternoon, if it was fine, they could have cake with afternoon tea, and they might be able to provide some "Forties music". Sam jumped at the chance, and promised to set up the PA system on the lawn in order to play the appropriate compact discs. He did this as a sort of rehearsal in two days' time after the usual Thursday night clapping at 8 pm. The staff did not let themselves get depressed by the news of 27,800 dead from Covid-19 by Thursday 30th April and 30,000 dead by 6th May.

The VE celebration on Friday 8th May is what happened. Stella found some union jack bunting that she looped across the tops of the windows facing the lawn. As soon as one of the teachers from the local primary school saw the bunting, she got the few pupils who still attended school each day (children of key workers) to make a very big cloth rainbow which Stella could spread over the lawn: the rainbow had become a symbol of hope through lockdown and most of the houses in Woodside Avenue had them displayed in their windows.

The trumpeter was delighted to be asked, and he signalled the start of the two minutes' silence with the "Last Post" at eleven, and the end of it with "Reveille". Many villagers came and stood in Woodside Avenue outside the fence for the silence, and at 3 pm afternoon tea was served on tables on the lawn for all the guests who wanted it. Sam's provision of music was perfect. He started with Vera Lynn singing "There'll be bluebirds over the white cliffs of Dover". Then he found a Glenn Miller recording of "In the mood", went on with Anne Shelton's "I'll be seeing you", Flanagan and Allen's "Run, rabbit, run", Gracie Fields' "Sally" and finishing with "We'll meet again". Sam and Nicky jogged together across the lawn, being joined by Chris and Lorna. At the end of the day, everyone was very tired and they were all very happy, as they watched the Queen's broadcast at 9 pm.

Chapter 9

It had been a happy time on VE day, and the established routine carried the impetus of life forward for the following week. During the Tuesday of the next week, 19th May, Stella and Jo sat in the office with their mid-afternoon tea. Afternoons were very quiet and sleepy now. Jigsaws and board games were quiet activities at the best of times, but now that no other visitors at all came on Tuesday, Wednesday and Friday afternoons, that made the weeks seem longer and more dull.

'That was a good day when we had the trumpet-player and the music that Sam put on during the afternoon. There was even a tiny bit of dancing on the lawn,' said Stella. 'Still, we can't expect all afternoons to be bright and lively, I suppose.'

'Apart from what enjoyment we make for ourselves, there's precious little else to cheer us up,' agreed Jo. 'Last Wednesday, 13th May, it was announced that total deaths from Covid were 33,682, and 6,000 people had died in care homes since the end of March.'

'I wouldn't trust the figures too much, Jo,' said Stella. 'How many of those care home deaths were caused by the virus is just not known: they have not all been virus-tested. You could add another 50,000 to those 33,000 if you wanted. I saw figures this morning showing that in normal years, between mid-March and the end of April, 100,000 people die. But this year, 150,000 died, and so what caused the extra 50,000 this year? Just because they were not tested as Covid-19 doesn't mean that they weren't. Plenty die untested in care homes. We know that Martin's death was not virus-related, but if we had said it was, it wouldn't have made any difference: it wouldn't have been recorded as such. What about all those people who died in their own homes? Doctors who attended them are so cavalier in what they will write on certificates. "Multiple organ dysfunction": what exactly does that mean? All deaths come down to that. "Broncho-pneumonia": well, that could easily be Covid, tested or not. I have even seen "Frailty" written on an elderly person's certificate. So, if you want to think the worst, you could add the 50,000 increase to the 33,000 and have over 80,000 deaths from the virus.' There was a pause, after nodded agreement. 'It does seem, though,' continued Stella, 'that the daily total has dropped to about three or four hundred from the previous eight or nine hundred a day. At least, that is what has been recorded. But I have seen other figures today which say that total deaths are now 41,000, with 11,000 in care homes. What is known is that between March and May 12,500 residents of care homes died, of whatever causes. You never know where you are with different sets of figures. I notice that yesterday, 18th May, scientists said that lack of taste or smell is now a symptom: they denied that two weeks ago.'

'No,' Jo agreed. 'All we can do is follow guidance, use our common sense, and take all the precautions we know we should.'

'And leave the rest to Providence,' smiled Stella.

'Providence of one sort or another,' said Jo.

'Still, what we can't do is get despondent. I must just think how lucky I am to have you here, and lucky that Maggie, Sam and Nicky said they would move in to help. Want another cup of tea?'

'Yes. Please, Stella.'

That seemed to draw a line under the disconsolate and downcast mood they had slipped into, and, without saying so, they wanted to neutralise it and sit calmly for a minute or two before they left the office, went downstairs and checked that all was well. At the same time, they would look round for other jobs that might need doing.

The calm lasted no more than two minutes. They heard a movement in the top corridor. Then the side door of the office opened. That door led into a corridor and then along past the two large "intermediate" bedrooms and the family bathroom a little further on. This bathroom was now being used by Maggie, in the nearest room, and by Sam and Nicky from downstairs. Now, Maggie stood, white-faced and looking in considerable distress. There were the stains of tears on her cheeks as she looked at Stella. She had not climbed the stairs, but had walked only three yards from the bedroom next door, and yet she was panting and seemed very short of breath. She was also holding her hand to the left side of her head.

'Oh, Stella, I think I'll have to give up,' she said. 'I feel dreadful. I didn't want any lunch today, and I've been lying down in my room, trying to get some rest, but I can't because I've got this stabbing headache and it seems to be all down the side of my head and face. Even my hair and the skin of my scalp are painful.'

'Well, has it suddenly come on since this morning, then?' asked Stella, a little taken aback.

'No. I've been trying to struggle on, knowing you were short-staffed, but I've had this horrible feeling, almost like 'flu, for about a week, and now I feel so tired and exhausted that I don't think I can go on. And this headache, I think it'll split my head open.'

Stella stood up, and although Maggie looked a pitiful sight, she resisted her natural urge to go over and give her comfort with an arm round her.

'I think you'd better go and lie down again, Maggie,' she said, full of a feeling of sympathy. 'Can you manage to get back onto the bed on your own?'

'I think so.' She panted as she seemed to push the words out, as tired as she was. She went slowly back.

Stella turned to look at Jo, who was looking back at her, hard, unwavering, suddenly alert and full of energy. 'Heavens, I don't like the look of this, Jo,' she said, picking up the phone.

'You're quite right. I don't like the sound if it, either,' said Jo.

'I'm dialling 111,' said Stella, 'but I'll bet I'll be hanging on for ages…..'Yes, there's a message saying I'm in a queue. Look, can I leave you holding on to the phone, Jo, and I'll go and make sure Maggie's comfortable, and I'll take her temperature.'

Stella looked no better when she returned. 'It's 39,' she said. 'This is serious, Jo,' and she took the phone.

'There's a queue of at least an hour,' said Jo. And Stella put the phone down.

'Right. Just check with me, Jo, as we go along. I've got a horrible feeling this is it. This is what we've been dreading. Maggie is not as old as the guests, but she's no Spring chicken, either. She's had this "flu-thing" for a week. Now she's got this strange headache and head pain. She's got a high temperature, doesn't want to eat, feels exhausted, and you could see how out of breath she was when she'd only walked three or four yards. She's had a cough, but not severe or persistent yet.' She paused and drew a deep breath. 'This is it, isn't it, Jo?' Jo nodded. 'Right. I can't wait all afternoon for the NHS on 111. This is not 999 – not yet. OK. I've got a direct line number for Dr Attwood. I've no idea what he's likely to be doing, but I'm going to interrupt. If I tell him the symptoms and my opinion, I can't be accused of covering up, keeping it to ourselves because we're a care home. Well, I'm absolutely certain he won't come here – far too busy, he'll say, apart from the obvious risk. Then he'll say that this call is our telephone consultation, and he'll go over the symptoms with me. He'll say I'm right to be worried about the temperature, and the most important thing at this moment and the most significant thing is to check the oxygen levels. At that point I will have anticipated him because I will have done it. Can you just try 111 again, Jo, while I go to Maggie and test her with the pulse-ox?'

Jo tried, knowing it would be hopeless, and it was, but Stella was soon back.

'That's not bad,' she said. 'It might be a teeny bit low, but nothing alarming. Thanks, Jo,' Stella continued as she took the phone back, stopped the call and rang Dr Attwood. He answered immediately. Stella put the phone on "Speaker" so that Jo could listen, and it went exactly as Stella had predicted.

He concluded: 'This does look ominous, Stella, but Brookfields are up to their eyes right now, and I'm going to leave this patient in your capable hands. You said she has no relatives within a hundred miles of Gainsford, so she is obviously in the best place for her. You don't need me to tell you to isolate her. But, Stella, you absolutely must check that oxygen level constantly. Take and record the reading at least twice a day, night and morning, and again during the day if you can. If it goes down, there's no messing about. It's 999, and please let me know when she's gone to the hospital. We'll leave it there at the moment.'

'Just as I thought,' said Stella when he'd finished the call. 'Can I just run past you the procedures I'm thinking of, Jo? The first thing is, I'll take her another cup of tea with Ibuprofen for her headache, and we'll see if it has any effect.

'I'll say that from now on, I, and only I, will attend to all Maggie's needs and I'll keep her in bed. I'll take her all her food, drinks and medication, and see to all her bed-linen needs, washing, showering and dressing if she needs it. Every time I go in, I'll wear full PPE, of course.

'Tell me what you think, Jo, but I'm proposing to move Maggie down into Martin's old room, number four. After his son had been here, and all his possessions had gone, I deep-cleaned the whole room and en-suite. I arranged fresh bed-linen. If I move her down there, as if she's one of the guests, that room can be sealed in the sense that Maggie will stay in it all day and all night, and only I will go in and out to see her for any other reason.'

Jo was beginning to frown as she listened, and so Stella explained. 'You see, Jo, if Maggie is in number four, she will use only that one toilet and shower. Upstairs, here, she's been sharing the bathroom with Sam and Nicky. Therefore, when she has moved downstairs, I will deep-clean all that "intermediate" room that she's been using, and get all the bed linen washed and replaced. Incidentally, I will also do all the laundry work myself from now on. It's not heavy, mostly pushing buttons. The servicing of rooms I will leave to you and Nicky, the individual medications to you.'

'Yes, I see,' said Jo. 'I suppose you have no option but to do all this, and the rest of us have no option but to let you.'

'Yes. The next priority is to tell Sam and Nicky exactly what the situation is. Neither of them should be busy half-way through a Tuesday afternoon, and they must be somewhere on the premises. I'll ask them if they would continue to use the same bathroom that they have been using upstairs here, and I will assure them that all Maggie's clothes, possessions and bathroom things and Maggie herself will be in Room four within the hour. I'll also ask them not to tell anyone else for the moment, though we will have to tell everyone as soon as is convenient; probably, I could tell everyone who is in breakfast tomorrow morning, and if we identify anyone not there, would you be responsible for finding them and telling them? Have I left anything out, Jo?' Stella finished with a bit if a sigh.

'No. I think you've covered everything for the moment, Stella. Everything seems to fall on you, but I don't think we have any option.'

'No. OK, then. Could you go and find Sam and Nicky, then, and if you could come with them up here, the four of us could chat about things and we'll give them all the reassurance we can. Oh, by the way, I can't see how to arrange things in any other way than Sam carrying on with all he does in the kitchen, and you, Nicky and I sharing all the shifts with the present arrangements being replaced by everything being "ad hoc". And no more all-night shifts. You and I have our pagers and the guests will have a button to press on their bedside cabinets. Agreed?'

'Yes. OK. Thank you,' said Jo. Her smile was one of admiration and thanks.

Sam and Nicky had not gone walking in the grounds, but they were sitting outside enjoying the Spring sunshine. They were therefore able to respond straightaway to Jo's message that Stella wanted all four of them to meet together in the office urgently. They exchanged puzzled glances, but hurried quickly behind Jo in through the kitchen lounge and up the central staircase. As they came into the office, Stella was just coming in through the door which led into the corridor with the two large bedrooms and the large bathroom.

'Thank you for coming quickly,' said Stella, 'but I have to give you some very serious news.' She rushed on without pause. 'What we have been dreading since we isolated, all through April and especially since Martin died, has happened. Jo and I think that Maggie is suffering with the corona virus. I've phoned the doctor. He thinks it's quite likely, but if so, she's not bad enough yet for us to call an emergency ambulance to take her to hospital. She has no relatives anywhere near and lives on her own when she's not here, so for the moment she'll have to stay here with us, and we'll look after her and constantly check her progress.

'She's in bed in there.' Stella pointed at the closed door, and meant the bedroom just the other side of it. I've been talking to her, and it seems that she's not been well for about a week with something that feels like bad 'flu. She's had a cough, but not too bad at present. She has a high temperature and seems very ill. I could kick myself for not noticing anything, but she says she's been struggling on because she didn't think it was serious, and she knew we were short-staffed and didn't want to let us down. What has happened is that we've been so busy watching the guests carefully for symptoms that it hasn't occurred to us to watch each other. If she's been feeling this bad all week and if she is infected, she's probably had it for two weeks now. It now seems, after talking to her, that she's had a sore throat for a few days. The symptoms don't appear for about four days or so. Even so, she hasn't had the most obvious symptom, a persistent, dry cough. Her cough is mild and occasional. I've had a look, and her throat is fairly bad. I have checked her oxygen levels, the best indicators, and they don't give any cause for alarm.' She drew a deep breath, but did not ask for questions.

'Right, so what I've decided to do is permanently move Maggie downstairs to Number four, Martin's old room. I have deep-cleaned and completely sanitised that room, and put in fresh bedding. Between now and supper time tonight, I am going to move all Maggie's possessions and everything she needs to live and put them in Number four. When everyone else is in the dining room and you are serving them, I'll take Maggie herself down. Then she will stay in that room day and night and never come out. Only I will go in and out with her food and drink and anything else she needs. She will use only the toilet, washbasin and shower in that en-suite.

'Meanwhile, I will also remove everything else from her old room up here on the first floor and take it down to the laundry. I will be doing all the laundry myself from now on. I will also deep-clean that room, and the bathroom next door that you use, including the toilet. I'll do that first, because I want you, if you will, to keep using that bathroom. Although I will saturate it with the strongest bleach we have, I don't think you are in danger using that bathroom. The reason why I say this is that, having studied all the information we have on the virus, it seems that with some patients, from entry into the body through the mouth, nose or eyes, and the virus having settled in the throat, it travels down the oesophagus to the stomach and digestive system, where it does not stay as long as in the lungs and makes a fairly quick exit, giving the patient diarrhoea. And the thing is' – and here Stella closed her fist and pumped it up and down – 'she has had diarrhoea and also has not told anyone. But the good news in all this is that – and this is only a guess – that it has not gone in such huge numbers down Maggie's trachea, bronchioles and alveoli, because that is when it is lethal. So we'll keep our fingers crossed about that, and hope that the heaps and heaps of strong bleach I plaster all over that toilet and bathroom will keep you safe. You are the youngest ones, of course, and your immune systems ought to be strong.' Stella paused and forced a smile. 'Will you do that, then?'

Sam and Nicky sat with perfect stillness while she spoke. Then, quietly, Sam said: 'Anything you want, Stella. We trust you completely.'

The new arrangements for running Woodside Lodge settled into a rhythm during the rest of the week, and Stella thought Maggie was stable. This rhythm coped with the stretching of resources which Stella had arranged, for now a spirit of "soldiering on" had taken hold of the skeleton staff of four even more tightly. There was a feeling of everyone braving the worst of it, which was fed by the events and by the figures which the media published each day and which showed the course of Covid. On Monday 25th May, one of the Prime Minister's advisers held a press conference on the lawn of No. 10, Downing Street, to explain why he had broken the lockdown regulations. On the Tuesday, the total number of UK deaths was announced at 37,048, and a total of only 180 deaths on that day was thought to be a sign of hope. But it went relentlessly on. On Wednesday 27th May, the total was 37,480 deaths with 470 on that day alone, and also on that day, tragedy struck again at Woodside Lodge.

Lunch had just been cleared away. Sam was making various arrangements in the kitchen. Stella had made sure the washing machines were working well in the laundry, and she had just joined Jo in the office for yet another cup of tea, but no-one knew where Nicky was.

They soon found out as she burst into the office. 'Oh, Stella. Dennis is in a bad way. I had noticed he wasn't at breakfast, but he has missed that a few times recently, and I've been too busy all morning to go and see him: there were four others not at breakfast, either.'

'But I've been calling into him at about half-past six each day, and he always answers cheerfully and says he's just going to get up,' said Stella.

'Yes, well he wasn't at lunch either, and when I just now went to check on him, he was dressed but sitting in a chair leaning forward, and coughing really vigorously. He was wheezing as he spoke to me, but he said he had been feeling worn out and tired, and today it seemed worse than ever. When I asked, he said he had not had a headache or diarrhoea, and he hadn't felt particularly hot or feverish, just every so often, tremendously tired. He sat down or lay on his bed, and after a while, he felt a bit better and carried on with his model-making. He then had another coughing fit and it sounded really bad.'

'Right!' Stella collected herself together. 'Nicky, can you phone 111? You probably won't get an answer. It'll just keep giving you messages until I get back, but if it does answer, would you tell the person exactly what you've told me, having first told them that we're a care home. If you can persuade them to keep the line open until I get back, do so, but I doubt it. Jo, would you come with me to see Dennis? If you get a thermometer, I'll get the pulse-oxymeter.'

There was no attempt to answer, just to do as Stella said, and then she and Jo were descending the wide staircase with all speed. They found Dennis just as Nicky had said. His temperature was a shade over 38, and his oxygen level, surprisingly, Stella thought, nothing to be alarmed about. He said he had taken his metformin every day, first thing in the morning. He had had a cough for three or four days, and had coughed nothing up, but today it seemed much worse. He had sat down most of the day making his models, and when he felt tired he went to lie down on his bed, and eventually had a little more energy. Jo looked down his throat and said it was inflamed. Dennis admitted that he had not gone out and got some exercise during the day, as Stella had kept telling him, but that was because he was so tired, and he hadn't wanted to bother Stella and Jo because the mild cough and the tiredness were all that was wrong. He was adamant that he did not want anything to eat, though Stella said she would send Nicky with a full pot of tea and would Dennis please drink it all, using his own cup and not one from the kitchen.

Nicky still had the phone clamped to her ear when the two ladies returned. She answered Stella's questioning look with a shake of the head.

'Would you take a full pot of tea down to Dennis, please, Nicky, but take no cup or saucer because I've told him he must use his own, and don't you bring it back later. Empty the teapot in his en-suite when he's finished, and leave that with him as well. Whenever you go in and out of his room from now on, Nicky, it's full PPE. Put it on now in my sitting room, where all we've got of it is, and I'll take a look at you before you go down.' There was no answer needed or given, and Stella turned to Jo: 'I'll ring Dr Attwood to record this, Jo. He'll say the same as with Maggie, and I'll promise to record Dennis's oxygen levels at least twice before his bedtime.

'Again, it's what happens when people think they won't bother us because they think we're too busy,' said Jo.

'Yes, although if he's only been coughing hard in the last day or two, and if that sore throat was mild enough to ignore, it's almost as if he was asymptomatic, because we all get tired.'

'It's a wonder how the virus gets in, though, when we are so carefully isolated.' Jo spoke her thoughts aloud.

'It can be anyhow,' said Stella. 'There's no telling. In Dennis's case, he gets a lot of small things by mail order, things like his balsa wood and glue and all the little fittings. I'll bet he doesn't wipe his small parcels down when he gets them, or quarantine the paper and materials before he uses them.'

'What about Maggie?'

'She gets things via couriers, too. I know she had many consignments of fresh bedlinen about a fortnight ago. She does quarantine all the material she gets, but I'm not sure how careful she is with the packaging, and the latest thinking is that the virus can live longer on inanimate things than we thought. Anyway, you can't live without taking some sort of risk, and so all any of us can do is follow the most secure ways of doing things we can think of, and hope that gets us through.'

When Stella rang Dr Attwood, the content of what he asked and said was much the same as for Maggie, but in one sense he was much more concerned about Dennis.

'If this patient has been asymptomatic, Stella, and the symptoms which are now suddenly developing are confined to the respiratory system, it could become extremely serious. If enough fluid starts to build up in the alveoli to send the immune system into overdrive, then it doesn't matter how many interferons, white blood cells, T-cells or anti-bodies are brought into play, his system could head straight to ARDS. If that is happening, it will be 999 and to A&E immediately. In fact, Stella, if that starts to happen and they say there's not an ambulance available, or they give you a time of, say, over twenty minutes, ring me and I'll come and drive your minibus to Brookfields, and if my presence gets him more quickly to triage, then they'll get him straight to intensive care. If it is as I say, that could be the killer. Intensive care people will have to decide on a ventilator or CPAP.'

All this had a strong effect on Stella. It was true that in Dennis's case, it had gone straight to his chest.

'Yes. Thank you, Dr Attwood. I'll be sure to get in touch if necessary.'

'What you absolutely must do, Stella,' he continued, 'is watch those oxygen levels like a hawk. My guess is that they may go down suddenly, although I hope it doesn't work out like that. I am confident that you know what you're doing, Stella, but keep in touch. 'Bye for now.'

Stella gave a bit of a blow of the lips when she had put the phone down, and Jo had been watching her intently all the time. 'It's OK. You hadn't put speaker mode on, but I heard all that last part anyway.'

Nicky had got a pot of tea ready, and stood watching and listening and waiting for Stella to send her down to Dennis.

'I think you had better put full PPE on, Jo, and take that tea down to Dennis,' said Stella. 'Make it clear to him that he doesn't leave his room day or night. I'll keep taking everything to Maggie, and if you can do the same for Dennis, always with full PPE on, that will make sure he doesn't speak to anyone else, but has all his food, drink and medication in there and does any washing or going to the toilet in his own unit. Sorry, Nicky, but Dr Attwood had a very urgent tone to all that he said at the end of the call, and I can see his point. ARDS is Acute Respiratory Distress Syndrome, Nicky, and if the virus is concentrating everything on his lungs, that's the direction in which he'll go.'

Jo had already gone into Stella's room to get the PPE on, and now emerged to take the teapot and a small jug of milk on a tray down to Dennis.

'Thanks, Jo,' said Stella, as Jo went quickly through the door and down the staircase. 'You'd better change back again, Nicky. Things are getting harder all the time, but I know what you're made of.' She smiled at Nicky, but then gave a big, long sigh.

At supper time, Dennis was his usual quiet, co-operative self. Jo could see that he had drunk his tea and washed and dried his own cup, saucer and teapot. He was indifferent towards food, but gladly accepted the soup Jo had brought him. Jo went round the room tidying, adjusting, dusting and polishing small objects here and there. She chatted light-heartedly to Dennis, who smiled gently in return. Jo had rather more affection for him than had Stella. He was such a quiet, unassuming man, who didn't mix with any enthusiasm with the other guests. He spent much of his time in his room, perfectly happy with his models: they absorbed so much of his interest. He was a bit of a dreamer. He read occasionally, and sometimes watched his TV, but often could be found looking quietly into space, apparently dreaming. Always, he was ready with that slow, gentle smile, almost as if he was reaching out for approval; he never complained or criticised other people, but was happy to live out a calm contentment. Stella, though, was critical of him, and said that if only he would take more exercise, as she was always urging him to do, he wouldn't continue to be registered as having type two diabetes.

By the time Dennis had finished his soup, Jo had been and fetched his supper, not giving him time to refuse, and he did not turn away when he saw it was a pasta salad that Sam had prepared. In fact, he ate the salad with something like relish, but left the pasta and Jo, who had stayed with him, disposed of it in his waste caddy and washed up for him. He also accepted a warm, milky drink which she offered to fetch, and that really pleased her. His oxygen levels were still a shade lower than they should have been.

All this meant that Jo could persuade Dennis that he needed, above all, to go to bed early. Although she was unable to touch him or to get too close, Jo did all she could to comfort him verbally, and then quickly went back to the office to take off her PPE, wash yet again and then go and eat a quick supper herself. She visited as many guests as she could before watching the TV in the kitchen lounge with three or four others, and then went in search of her own makeshift bed in Stella's sitting room.

Stella went through into her own bedroom when she saw that Jo wanted to go to bed early, and, indicating the PPE Jo had hastily discarded earlier, said that most of it was re-usable, and would have to be because their supplies of it were low, in spite of the fact that a new order had been repeatedly sent in.

Jo knew it would have to be re-used within a few hours, because Dennis would be her first port of call in the morning. However, when, suitably dressed, she opened Dennis's door at 6.30 am. the next day, his light was already on, which was most unusual. Even more unusual was the fact that he was out of bed, not dressed, but sitting on the side of the bed and coughing for quite a long span, until he calmed down and stopped.

He tried to tell Jo he had been out of bed and coughing for much of the night. His voice, though, was only a hoarse whisper, and he could give her the information only in little bursts of a few words at a time. Jo fetched him a drink of water from his shower room and waited for him to calm down. Meanwhile, she asked him why he hadn't pressed the button on his bedside cabinet, which would have buzzed her pager during the night. He did not answer, but when he was calmer, he began to shiver a little, and he needed no persuasion for him to get back into bed. Then Jo fetched him another drink to enable him to take his metformin tablet that she had brought him. Dennis knew that Jo would insist on his eating some breakfast, and so, without any resistance, he asked for Weetabix with plenty of milk. Jo was pleased at that because it could be prepared and brought in a short time. As it was still early, she could fetch that and then leave Dennis to himself, so that she could get the PPE off quickly and not march up and down the corridor wearing it for the other guests to see. Dennis became more like his usual self once he was eating his breakfast, so Jo left him alone, making a mental note to go back and check his oxygen level once breakfast was over.

Thursday was not a day when Sam provided a hot breakfast option, which meant that it was over reasonably quickly, although when there was no hot provision, some guests would come late and slowly to the dining room. Even then, the number wanting toast and tea or coffee at the end of the meal could prolong it. Today, though, Nicky, having been aware of the worry about Dennis yesterday, told Jo that she would see to the toast and tea afterwards. So, after eating a dish of cereal very quickly and swallowing a lukewarm cup of coffee, Jo donned her protective gear again while most of the guests were still lingering in the dining room.

When she entered Dennis's room, she saw immediately that he had only half-eaten his Weetabix and was lying back on his pillows. Through the hoarse whisper again, Dennis told Jo that he had been coughing again and felt worn out already.

'Does it hurt when you cough, Dennis?' Jo asked.

He nodded quickly and vigorously. Then he whispered that inside his chest, everything felt heavy, as if it was weighing him down, but he wanted to cough all the time because it seemed solid, and he couldn't breathe deeply enough. He wanted to get rid of whatever was in there. When he lay his head back on the pillow and turned to face Jo again, she noticed how tired and lined his face seemed to be. He was very pale, but under his eyes were dark shadows.

His appearance and attempted talk were but a preparation for the true situation Jo was looking for, because when she took the oxygen reading, she gave a little gasp. She told Dennis that she would be back quickly if he could wait a couple of minutes.

Jo hated having to move quickly in an ungainly way along the corridor, with the PPE awkwardly restricting her progress, and so she went out of the door at the end of the far corridor where No. 15 was situated. This meant that she could turn and trundle across the car park to the door by the laundry, go in there and through the laundry lounge, and so on up the main staircase. At the top, she bundled herself through the door and silently thanked God Stella was there.

'Stella, it's Dennis. 999. It must be. The oxygen level has fallen right down.'

'OK, Jo. I don't need to check if it's you telling me that.' She hesitated a milli-second. 'Yes. I'll ring for the ambulance first, and then Dr Attwood after that, if it's a long time for the ambulance.'

The person receiving the emergency call answered immediately and said they would send an ambulance straightaway. They would be at Woodside Lodge in under ten minutes, she told Stella. Stella put down the phone and rang Dr Attwood's direct line at the surgery. She said the ambulance would be there quickly and she was just informing him. He thanked her but said he would also ring the hospital so that they knew of the situation before Dennis's arrival, and he would give the oxygen level reading and the temperature and blood pressure readings of the day before, Wednesday 27th May. He thought it might speed things up.

Jo was still in her PPE, and, once Stella had finished with the telephone, Jo gave her a brief account of the events that morning. Stella nodded at each short stage, and then told Jo she had done exactly the right thing. Jo, dressed as she was, was the only person who could take the paramedics to Dennis's room and assist at that point. Stella went down and out of the laundry door to direct the incoming ambulance round and through the car park to the door at the end of the corridor. The ambulance arrived exactly ten minutes later, and with Jo's assistance, Dennis's transfer from his room to the ambulance was effected rapidly and smoothly.

As the ambulance moved away, Jo stood at the point where she had just helped load Dennis in and watched, steadily and sadly. Vivid pictures of her care for him the evening before, ran through Jo's mind. Calm and still though she was on the outside, tears pricked the backs of Jo's eyes as she watched. Poor Dennis, she thought; why is it always the gentle, loving ones?

Stella had to go back inside and telephone Dennis's daughter, who was next of kin. Then there was a room to clear, to parcel up Dennis's belongings, including his precious models, and then to deep-clean, sanitise, and refresh with clean laundry.

Chapter 10

O y! – Oy! – I want you!' It was Barbara at the dining room door, while breakfast was being served. 'You!' repeated Barbara more loudly. 'You – it's you I want!' She was pointing at Nicky.

Very few of the guests at Woodside were rude or abrupt with staff, but Barbara was the worst. Matt was sometimes a bit gruff because he was very deaf and, in spite of his hearing aid, he had a habit of leaning towards anyone speaking to him because he couldn't quite catch what they had said. Margery could be blunt and slightly aggressive in her manner of speaking – Stella thought it came from a defensive attitude because she had in the past suffered offensive comments about her being overweight. But if there was something Barbara didn't like, she could be short-tempered and aggressive, as she was being now. She was pointing at Nicky as she spoke. Nicky happened to be serving cereal to a table of four men – Lew, Vic, Mick and Matt – but that did not inhibit Barbara at all. She wanted something and she was going to interrupt anyone no matter what they were doing, and insist that she get it. She had done it with Nicky before. There were only ever two staff at meals nowadays, because Stella was dealing exclusively with Maggie, and now that Jo had been released from her constant attention to Dennis, she and Nicky were serving breakfast on Monday morning. Barbara, like all bullies, would attack whoever she perceived to be the more vulnerable target, and that had to be Nicky simply because she was young and Barbara thought she was more likely to get what she wanted.

As Nicky was serving the table of four, however, she did not answer but glanced across at Jo. Unfortunately for Barbara, Jo was capable of handling any situation.

'Never mind who you want, what do you want, Barbara?' Jo cut in.

'I said I want her,' insisted Barbara, rudely, belligerently, loudly.

'You can see Nicky is busy, as well as I can.' Jo raised her voice, implying that she was not going to be shouted down, or swept aside. 'Whatever you want, I will be able to deal with, so – what – is – it?'

It was clear that Barbara was in something of a hurry, and she quickly decided to engage with Jo. 'Would you come, please?' The tone had softened. 'It's Ella. I'm worried, really worried. Would you come, please?'

Jo had finished with her table for the moment, and moved very quickly and urgently to the door, where Barbara still stood. Jo walked straight through the doorway, and Barbara had no option but to follow her into the kitchen lounge.

'It's Ella.' Barbara was quick and direct now. 'She's refusing to get up out of bed and come to breakfast. She says she's too tired and can't be bothered. It was the same last night. I had to practically drag her to supper last night, but now she's worse and I can't make her budge.'

'Come on!' Jo set off at some speed, and they talked as they headed past the front door into the laundry lounge and across that to No. 5.

'I know she can be awkward and impulsive, and she forgets things all the time, but she usually lets me take her to where she needs to be,' Barbara said.

'Yes. We know she's difficult, Barbara.' Jo's tone of voice was really quite friendly now. 'Stella and I are very grateful for the way you look after her. She's not an easy guest to have in here, because the GP refers everything to the hospital and the neurologists are not quite sure about the state of her brain. She suffers from something between Alzheimer's and Parkinson's, probably Lewy Bodies dementia. That's why she drools all the time. Can't help it. Anyway, let's see.'

Jo pushed open the door, entered the room, and her brisk manner totally and instantly changed. She smiled as she approached Ella. 'Now, Ella,' she said, almost caressing her with the soft tone of her voice. 'Barbara tells me you don't want to come to breakfast.' It was a statement of fact, but the tone was that of a question.

Ella lay back on her pillows. 'Can't be fagged.' That was one of a few expressions she had which meant 'tired' or 'fed up'. Jo grabbed two tissues from the bedside cabinet and took some time to wipe and clean Ella's nose. 'I know I'm in a mess, but I've been coughing and spluttering a lot,' said Ella, looking up submissively into Jo's face.

'You're alright. You can't help it.' Jo was reassuring and gentle.

'Under your tongue,' she said as she pulled a sanitised thermometer from the breast pocket of her uniform. While she waited, Jo looked quickly around the untidy clutter of the room, and went into the en-suite. She found a spoon which she put under the tap which ran as hot as she could get it. Back in the room, she looked at the thermometer: 38.5. She shook it, wrapped it in a small cloth which just fitted it, and replaced it in her top pocket. 'Why did Barbara have to persuade you to go for supper last night?'

'Just forgot.' Jo glanced at Barbara, who pulled a face and slightly shook her head.

'Come on. Open,' said Jo, as she slipped in the warm spoon and rapidly looked at Ella's throat. 'Go and wash that and leave it in there,' Jo said curtly, as she passed the spoon to Barbara, and then turned back to Ella. 'Now, Ella,' she said, and the friendly, caressing tone had gone from her voice. 'I'm going to send Barbara back in here with a dish of Weetabix with warm milk.' Jo had now raised her voice a little, and it had that sharp, commanding tone that all the guests associated with the blue uniform.

Ella was not going to make anything of it. 'I'll try,' she said, softly.

'Just lie back there, and keep warm,' Jo said, slightly more softly.

'OK,' There was a short spasm of coughing, and Ella lay back.

Jo made for the door, pushing the little button that all the doors had, which illuminated a "Do not disturb" sign outside. She beckoned to Barbara, and they both slipped out and quickly walked away. There was no more need to talk. Barbara had heard Jo's instructions, and when they reached the foot of the staircase, she continued into the kitchen lounge, and then through the dining room into the kitchen to do as Jo had asked. Nicky looked in through the door, an unspoken question on her face. 'Jo told me to take some Weetabix to her and leave it outside her room,' said Barbara.

Meanwhile, Jo went up the stairs, through the office, and turned left into the sitting room, where Stella was just finishing her own breakfast. Jo began putting on her PPE, while she was speaking, because she hadn't had chance when she left the dining room.

'Good morning, Stella,' said Jo, who had not seen her until now, although she knew she had been downstairs attending to Maggie. She was answered with a smile and a nod.

'Ella's giving some concern.' Jo came straight to the point. 'She wouldn't go to breakfast when Barbara tried to get her to go. It was the same last night, so she's obviously off her food. She also has a temperature – 38.5 – and a sore throat, as well as saying she is too "fagged", as she puts it, to get up. She has, though, been coughing during the night, and I've heard her just now. It did not sound good.'

'H'm,' said Stella, tightening her lips. 'Well, could I ask you to go back down and get a 'pulse-ox' reading, Jo? This the fourth day since they took Dennis in. By the way, I've had a message that he went into intensive care on Saturday.

CPAP. They didn't think he could stand up to a ventilator. His daughter has come to Gainsford, but, obviously, they won't let her visit. Anyway, I'll wait for the 'pulse-ox' reading, Jo, and then I'll phone Dr Attwood. He won't come, and, although I'll tell him the symptoms, he won't do or say anything except to refer her to Brookfields, who know her well, and have all her records. But I'll let him decide whether it's 999, or a straightforward admission, and he can do it. It'll depend on the pulse-oxymeter reading, so if you could get that done before I ring him, Jo, please.'

Jo called Stella's pager from Ella's room, and then spoke by phone. 'Oxygen is down – 92' was the message. 'The breakfast is here, and I'm going to try to make her eat it and drink a glass of water.'

'Right. Thank you. I'll ring Attwood. Let's hope we've caught Ella in time,' said Stella.

Dr Attwood reacted exactly as Stella said he would and, having consulted the hospital, he rang back quickly. They would admit Ella, he told her; they were not prioritising her, but hoped to get an ambulance to Woodside sometime during the morning.

'Yes. At least she's been eating and drinking while I've been standing over her,' said Jo, as she returned. 'I am afraid she's beginning to sweat now, though. I've left her dish and drinking glass down there, and told her to make sure she keeps them. Don't know why I bothered to say anything, though, because she started asking me why I was all dressed up, and where was Barbara? She's already forgotten about early this morning, let alone last night.'

'Yes. Well, the ambulance is coming as soon as they can get here this morning, so you'll have to keep your PPE on until then, and deal with the paramedics, please, Jo. Perhaps you can speed things up by getting all her personal things collected together and ready for them. I'll keep a lookout from the kitchen lounge window, and nip out to direct them. The laundry door will be the nearest to No. 5.'

The ambulance did not come until about half past eleven, and so there was a bit of waiting around to be done. Jo had plenty to do, gathering Ella's personal belongings and making sure she had all she would need in the hospital, assuming she was in for a reasonably long stretch. She also tried to tidy everything ready for Stella's sanitising blitz on the unit once Ella was on her way. Jo thought she might have some comforting and reassuring to do with Ella, but she seemed to take it all very calmly, got into a set of clean pyjamas while Jo was busy, and then sat and waited as if she was a small girl going on her holidays. That only added to the poignancy for Jo.

Stella was feeling similarly in flat spirits as she watched through the laundry lounge window, having waved the ambulance through to the laundry door. She began to have a feeling of slow inevitability as she watched Jo in full PPE attending the paramedics as they loaded the trolley/stretcher into the ambulance, and then handing in three substantial bags for Ella to take with her. She had had to wipe her damp eyes when Dennis had left just four short days ago, but now it was a dull ache that gripped her throat as the ambulance drove slowly past the window, and she turned to go and telephone Ella's family.

She had only reached the foot of the staircase before going up to the office, when Barbara stood in front of her, wanting to speak.

'Ella's going into hospital, isn't she, Stella?'

'Yes, Barbara. I'm afraid so. They'll give her the treatment that she needs, and we can't give,' said Stella, feeling sorry for Barbara, as she stood fidgeting with the arms of her cardigan.

'Is she going to Brookfields?'

'Yes.'

'Can you tell me the ward, so that I can go and visit her?' asked Barbara.

Stella realised the situation immediately. Barbara's emotional reaction to Ella's departure had prevented her understanding the full situation.

'I doubt whether they will let you visit, Barbara, and I don't know the ward yet. In any case, even if the hospital allowed you to go, I would have to say you can't.'

Stella saw the shock on Barbara's face as she suddenly understood what Stella meant.

'What? Why can't I visit? She needs me,' she blurted out. Stella realised she would have to explain patiently.

'Oh, Barbara, if we are locked down, we have to isolate properly and completely. No-one can go in or out, and that includes you wanting to visit Ella.'

'But she needs me,' Barbara called out in a shrill tone. The tension had not moderated. 'I know Ella. She's my friend. I can tell the hospital all sorts of things about her, how she has trouble going to the toilet, how she's slow to get moving and can only take little steps because she feels stiff a lot of the time, how sometimes she feels cold but then suddenly she's sweating and feels dizzy. And, of course, she can never remember anything, and all that drooling – oh, I'm always wiping her clean, but it's not her fault. She can't help it, you know. I could tell them all these things. I want to be with her and help her.' All this came tumbling out from Barbara, in breathless profusion.

'Oh, no, Barbara.' Stella tried to sound understanding, and had to resist the feeling that she needed to put her arm around her. 'Ella may well be seriously ill, and only the qualified, expert people can look after her. They already know all about her, and they know everything you are saying. But because they are looking after her very closely, I'm afraid they can't let you help, and I can't let you go from here.'

Barbara would not calm down or be pacified. 'But I must go, I must go, and I'm going, whatever you say, Stella. I'm going.' She was shrieking, and obviously was not going to listen.

'Please understand, Barbara,' Stella remonstrated again, 'I cannot let you go, and, wherever Ella is, you cannot visit her. It's no good you upsetting yourself. That's how it is with the hospital, and that's how it is with me.'

'Well, I won't have it, I won't have it!' Barbara was shouting. She would not see the situation from any perspective except her own. She strutted into the laundry lounge for about five yards and then strutted back again, stamping. Stella looked at her, slightly shaking her head, at a loss as to how to persuade her to leave it at that.

'Ella is my friend, my best friend,' Barbara continued, unabated. 'The most important thing for me is to find where she is, and go there to be with her and help look after her.' She stopped, glaring at Stella, waiting for a reply, but Stella just looked, and gave a little shrug.

Barbara was also now frustrated in her attempts to persuade Stella, and so she threw her arms in the air and marched off through the laundry lounge to her room. 'Well,' she called back as she went away, 'if I can't go and see her and stay living here, then I'll leave here and then go and see her. I'll phone my son-in-law. He'll come and fetch me and I'll move out to live with my daughter. They've no children, and they'll have me.'

That's how it worked out. When Barbara had phoned her daughter, Mary, she rang Stella to ask what it was all about. When Stella had explained, Mary agreed that nothing could be done about it. She sighed deeply, and, in a tone of resignation, agreed to take Barbara in and look after her. Mary's husband came in a van the next day, waited until Stella and Barbara had collected together and placed, on the path outside the front door, all Barbara's possessions. Then he loaded them all in, came and apologised to Stella about the whole thing, asked for a final account invoice, led Barbara by the hand down the path, and packed her, too, in the front passenger seat. Then they drove off. Barbara did not wave or look back. There were no tears or aching throat from Stella this time. She had done her best for Ella and Barbara, and she could only do so much.

It was just after midnight towards the end of that week, on the night of Thursday 4th June, that Stella's pager beeped. She had not been to sleep and was out of bed and throwing on her dressing gown immediately. Jo must have been in the same position, because as Stella approached the door, Jo, who slept in the sitting room, opened it. She must have heard it, too.

'Do you want me to go, Stella?' she asked.

'If you don't mind, Jo, yes. I would like you to come with me,' replied Stella. 'It's number twelve, so that's Matt, and it's likely to be his heart. Do you remember giving him his beta-blocker today?'

'Yes, and he seemed OK. I haven't noticed him having any Covid symptoms, either.'

'Well, if he's short of breath, it's not going to do his heart any good. Right. I'll take the defibrillator if you'll get a thermometer and the pulse-oximeter.'

Within half a minute, they were through the sitting room, the office, and going down the staircase. 'I'm going to ring Attwood tomorrow to check if it's OK for Maggie to come out and get back to normal now. Counting the week before we isolated her, when she would have been positive, she's just on three weeks, so if Matt's got any Covid, it'll make no difference me coming.' They had to go through the laundry lounge, where Nicky had been sleeping, but she now stirred and watched. Then they went through the laundry, then down the corridor and round the corner to No. 12. They found Matt sitting on the bed in his pyjamas, clutching his chest.

'Got a pain?' Jo asked, reaching for his wrist to feel for a pulse. A few seconds' silence. 'H'm. It's there, but hard to count because it's not clear or firm. Could you just lean forward, Matt, and take some deep breaths?'

Matt shook his head. 'Hurts to lean forward. Can't take deep breaths. Hardly any breath at all.'

Stella cursed under her breath and she felt his wrist. Between them, they set and used the defibrillator. Matt lay still on the bed afterwards. He was quieter.

The two nurses looked at each other with set, hard faces and pursed lips. Stella felt the wrist again.

'It's a bit clearer, but it's not strong. We won't rush things. Do you want a drink, Matt?'

'Just a sip, yes.' Jo had already half-filled his glass in the en-suite. Matt gripped it tightly, and took many sips.

'Still a pain?' Matt nodded.

'Bad?' Another nod.

'I just can't get my breath. Can't draw it in,' he complained. 'It feels all solid down there. I'm suffocating.'

'Wait till he's calmer,' said Stella. 'We'll also try to get the heart-rate down. It's well over a hundred. But I'm really concerned about how shallow his breathing is. That's enough to keep him tensed up on its own.'

Stella went into the en-suite briefly, and returned with a warm spoon. She depressed Matt's tongue and looked briefly down his throat. 'Not too good,' was her judgment.

As he calmed, Jo took his temperature. 'Thirty-eight and a half,' she said, and held his hand. He was more still and less tense now.

After a short time, Stella said, 'He's a bit steadier now, but we can't leave him, with what we've done. I think there might be more factors than just his heart, and I think he's going to need more oxygen than we can give, so we'll do the 999.'

There was a prompt answer, and a promise to come immediately.

'I'll go and send them round to the other door,' said Stella.

'I'll do what I can to get him ready,' said Jo, 'but they'll have to take him from in here.'

'Yes. OK.'

Ten minutes later, Stella went out to direct the paramedics to the far door, and then retreated inside to watch through the laundry lounge window, as Jo waited for them and took them in. They carried a defibrillator, too. Nicky, having got up from her bed and got dressed, stood a little distance away, watching, talking in subdued tones to Stella.

'Was your Dad one of them that's gone in?' Stella asked.

'No. He's not a paramedic. He works part-time for Borrett's, the undertakers. By the time he and Jim Borrett get to where they've been called, the doctor's gone, the paramedics, if they came, have gone, too, and there's usually just a lone policeman there to make sure things are not disturbed. He would come if all that had happened here, during the night.'

'Yes. I'm sure I've seen him.'

After another short silence, the stretcher party re-emerged, they drove off with Matt, and everyone returned to their beds.

During the following morning, on the Friday, Stella telephoned Dr Attwood at the surgery to let him know about Matt, to enable him to update his records. She asked him to update Maggie's records, too, because earlier on the Thursday, Stella had told Maggie that she thought she could safely come out of isolation, her body having fought the infection for at least three weeks, probably four, and she was quite strong again. They came to an arrangement whereby Maggie would start to do her laundry work again, but not socialise with the guests in lounges or dining room, and would take her meals in her room, which would remain Martin's old room, No.4. Dr Attwood agreed with Stella's handling of the Maggie situation and also agreed that she had done exactly the right thing the night before with Matt.

'You absolutely must get oxygen to an ailing heart,' he said. 'Otherwise, it has nothing to go on. The paramedics have equipment in the ambulance, but only the hospital can permanently provide for people with weakening hearts. I understand that Brookfields is bursting at the seams again,' he added, 'but an emergency is an emergency.'

'We seem to have been sending a number of our residents to them recently,' said Stella. 'Two of our men and one of our women have been admitted in recent weeks, and now Matt makes four.'

'Yes. Well, being a care home like yours, you are bound to be on the front line,' continued the doctor. 'All your residents are by definition elderly and therefore vulnerable. I'll just explain something else to you about the present situation, Stella, and that is that, whereas people can die of Covid, an awful lot more can die of another complaint along with Covid. When you add to that the number of old people who died undiagnosed in their own homes, their deaths being attributed by doctors who signed the certificate to bronchial pneumonia or heart failure, there is no relying on the statistics at all. Those extra 50,000 deaths this year could well have been victims of the virus as well.'

'There's another dimension to all this as well, Stella. There are other viral ailments that sweep across the world annually or from time to time, and sometimes they mutate and sometimes they don't. They either kill their victims or are seen off by the anti-bodies and white blood cells, but what most have in common is that, having struck the victim, they or their offspring move on and the victim dies or recovers. With this, though, there is what some are calling a "long Covid". It seems to move about in the body from one organ to another, and the phrase "organ failure" could refer to the kidneys, liver, lungs, pancreas, heart, intestines and bowel, anywhere. It can even sleep for a period of time and then re-emerge a long time later. All these aspects, Stella, have to be borne in mind.'

'Yes,' replied Stella, wanting to draw the conversation to a close, 'but all the foot-soldiers like us can do is our best according to each case that comes in front of us.'

'M'm.' The doctor seemed to be finishing speaking as well, and then suddenly said, 'Oh, have you been notified about Dennis this morning?'

'No.'

'I expect they're busy and will inform you and tell the family later. He died during the night.'

'Oh, and what are they ascribing it to?'

'Don't know.'

As Stella put the phone down, her spirit wilted. She was very fond of Dennis – such a quiet, gentle man, absorbed in his modelling.

Stella told Jo after lunchtime, drinking tea at 2pm. They shared a few moments of emptiness, and then sadness. Then Stella said, 'That's four gone recently, then: Martin, Dennis, and now Ella and Barbara, and I expect Matt will soon join them. That will be five. It'll make a big hole in our finances, Jo.'

'Can't you do anything about it?'

'I've advertised, but had no response, and quite honestly, I didn't expect any. Families are not going to send their grannies and grandads into care homes in the present circumstances. They think we are hotbeds of infection.

'But, you know, I was talking on the phone to the manager of another residential home only yesterday, and she told me that they have had five of their residents die in the last three months, and they have made no attempt to replace them for fear of importing the virus. She said they were not going to. They must have been left some large legacies, I expect.'

'Intermediates?' asked Jo, after a short pause.

'Yes. I'm surprised we've not had any up to now,' said Stella. 'I'm sure they'll come. Under normal conditions I wouldn't want them, but now I think I'll have to. I'll tell you what, Jo, could you hold the fort for an hour this afternoon, please? I feel a bit weighed down, and I want to get out into the air for a time. I won't go on any public footpaths or come into contact with anybody else, but if I go to our boundary straight out of the back here, there is the wood after which this road is named. There is a small gate right over in the corner, and without being seen, I'm going to slip through that and walk in the wood for an hour. Will you cover for me?'

'Certainly,' said Jo. 'I'll tell anyone who asks that I don't know where you are, and then I'll see to whatever is bothering them.' She looked at Stella hard and seriously for a few seconds. 'Keep your spirits up, Stella.'

Chapter 11

Stella walked slowly and steadily down the staircase, through the laundry lounge, the laundry itself, out of the door and through the car park. She was glad no-one called to her or wanted anything and that she could make free progress. It was a very warm June day, and the warmth wafted towards her, urged forward by a gentle breeze. She walked with eyes half-closed, enjoying the warmth as it was tenderly pressed over her face and through her hair.

When she had crossed the lawns, she wandered loosely through the shrub area. It seemed only a very short time ago that Sid, who thought he still worked for the Parks and Public Gardens department of Gainsford District Council, had adored his beloved snowdrops and had enthused lyrically about the crocuses, daffodils and polyanthus that were replacing them in the Spring. She stole a quick glance behind her to make sure none of the guests saw her slip out and into the wood.

She felt the weight of responsibility for the residents of Woodside Lodge more heavily than she had done before. Within the space of two months, there were two men dead and a third well on the way, one lady in hospital and another having left apparently in sympathy. Stella did not just record the facts in her books; she felt them on her heart. Her mind coped with clinical efficiency, but her feelings operated more deeply and slowly.

Stella closed her eyes and surrendered herself to the cleansing power of the fresh air, the sun and the beauty of the natural world. As she began to walk through the wood, the mantle of the interlaced branches and the caressing touch of the breeze softened the heat of the sun. The path ahead was barred by the speckled shade of the birches. Further on was Stella's favourite part: a dark, latticed mesh was formed by the hazels so that little sunlight penetrated. In the dark and cool of the middle of the wood, Stella sat on a fallen log, closed her eyes and listened to the sound of Spring. There were the mellow, melodic tones of the blackbirds and from high above the canopy came the clear, strong, repetitive calls of the song thrush. And flitting about, plucking insects from the tender Spring foliage were the slender, elegant warblers – the staccato rise and fall of the chiffchaff, the delicate descending cadences of the willow warblers, and the bubbling harmonies of the blackcaps. Stella let the peace of the moment wash over her, and allowed the whistling innocence of birdsong to soothe her. The natural freshness of everything fed her spirit as she sat.

Sometime later, she got up from her seat and slowly walked back the way she had come. She felt renewed and refreshed. A new strength had seeped into her mind and body and she felt herself smiling again. She walked back the width of the wood, through the gate, unseen, and she moved serenely through the flower-filled gardens and across the coolness of the lawns.

As she approached the Lodge, there was no feeling of getting to grips with anything, overcoming any illness or resuming control: she just wanted to continue loving everything – the building and all the people inside.

Jo had been watching for Stella's return through the window of the corridor past the first units. She went out of the nearest door and hurried to meet Stella in the car park.

'I've admitted two intermediates in your absence, Stella. Brookfields hospital rang about half an hour after you'd gone. They wanted us to take a man and a woman who had both had the coronavirus, but had now regained their strength, and need some further care from us to recover. They needed to free-up two beds for new cases. I asked if they had been tested, and they said they had run out of what test material they had. I didn't know if you would have refused them if they hadn't been tested, Stella, so I agreed that they could come and they were here within half an hour. They are John and Eleanor, and we have installed them in the two guest bedrooms on the first floor just across the office from us, and I expected that we would have to look after them.'

'That's alright, Jo. There's never enough test equipment for an ideal amount of testing anyway, and I wouldn't have wanted to refuse. Thank you. You did the right thing. Now that we haven't got Matt and now that Maggie is well-recovered and doing her job in the laundry again, that releases both of us to look after these two. Did they give you their details?'

'Yes. I've got their records, and their present state of progress is there in writing. They have both been recovering for over a week, but Eleanor is diabetic and so is John, but John is also overweight and has a heart condition.'

'Details of medication?'

'Yes. It's all written in their records.'

'OK. Thank you. That will be quite a task for us. Let's get back to the office so that I can meet them and we can work out a personalised care plan, as we do for all the others, and that will show that we are treating everyone the same. First, though, Jo, would you do me the favour of finding Sam and Nicky, and asking them to come up to the office, so that they know all about the new situation, and can decide whether they want to carry on.'

'Right. See you in a few minutes, Stella.'

Sam and Nicky, who were both together in the kitchen lounge, came upstairs immediately and followed Jo into the office.

'Thanks for coming,' said Stella, as they sat down. 'We need to plan together to decide where we go from here. We have admitted two intermediates, people who have been ill, in this case with Covid-19. The hospital has given them all they need for the specific treatment for their condition, and they require further bed-rest and care from us to recover fully. Under the present circumstances, hospitals need absolutely all their beds and cannot have any blocked. The Council pays us to look after them temporarily from their social funds.' She paused, expecting questions, but as there were none, she continued. 'Now obviously this increases the danger that we four and Maggie and our guests are in. I am going to try to carry on, but I have no right to assume that you three, Jo, Nicky and Sam, are going to do the same. The decision is yours, and I will try to tell you all I can about the position we are in. By the way, if you didn't know, Maggie is better and at the moment, she will be up to her eyes in laundry work again, so I'll let her know later.'

Stella was calm, and was feeling the benefit of her walk. She paused again and took two deep draughts of water from the glass she had got for herself. 'If anyone wants a drink, help yourself,' she said, before continuing. 'The evidence is that, in spite of all we have done to isolate ourselves, we have the Covid virus in Woodside Lodge. Martin's death was nothing to do with it and we just don't know about Matt, because his heart was quite bad, but the symptoms shown by Maggie, Dennis and Ella were, I think, convincing. By the way, Sam and Nicky, we have heard today that, sadly, Dennis has died. And now, we are deliberately taking in two people that we know have suffered from it, but because they have not been tested in the last day or two, we cannot be sure.

'We have not got the equipment or material to test them ourselves. We've tried to get some but can't, and we get no help from the Department of Health. All that we hear about a protective arm round the care homes is nonsense. We don't get help. I study the reports of epidemiologists on the internet, and I listen to news bulletins. It seems that some people spread the virus quickly, others don't and we don't know why there is the difference: some conditions allow its spread. It seems there is a 1 in 10 chance of catching it from someone you live with, a 1 in 20 chance of catching it from someone you work with. You would have thought more, but those are the figures. It seems that younger people are not so vulnerable as older ones, and men are more susceptible than women, but we don't know why, and so much is unknown. If you decide to stay, the arrangement will be that the two new people will stay in those two guest rooms on the first floor. They have their own bathroom, and Jo and I will feed them. They will never come down to the ground floor.

'As I say, it is up to you whether you want to go home now and put your safety first or to stay here and help me run this place. I have no right to assume that any of the three of you want to stay here. Sam, you live on your own, and you, too, Jo, when your husband is away, and so you two should be going to safe places. You, though, Nicky, could possibly be taking something back to your family.'

Nicky interrupted with a stronger assertion than she normally did. 'But it's because I'm putting their safety before mine that I've already decided to stay. If I have got, or if I get, anything, I deliberately decided to stay here when we locked down, and I'm going to live with it. I'm not going to endanger my family by possibly taking an infection into the house.'

'I agree entirely with Nicky, and I'm staying, too.' Sam spoke before anyone else had a chance. 'How could you think that I would ever run away, Stella?' Sam and Nicky exchanged meaningful glances.

Stella closed her eyes. The gratitude that she felt towards these two young, brave people, she could not express adequately. 'Thank you,' was all she said, and it was heartfelt.

'I am the same,' Jo joined in. 'I'm staying to support you, Stella. Let me just say to Sam and Nicky, two young people who are just starting in this industry and who could just as easily work somewhere else, for Stella and me, who have been medically trained, this is not just a job. We don't just do this for money. It's not a job; it's a vocation. We give ourselves to this care home and its residents. It's not just a living; it's our lives.'

'Oh, yes,' agreed Stella. 'If we were a business interested only in profit, with five customers out of eighteen gone and not replaced, I would have to close down. My parents left me this building, but I have made the business what it is, with the help of people like Jo, and you two, and I'm not closing. I'm giving myself to it. This is what I am and what I do.'

A period of quiet followed, in which they all looked round at each other. Finally, Stella seemed to collect herself together. 'Well, if that's what you've all decided, thank you again, and now we'll just have to get on with things. I haven't even met the new residents yet, though I know plenty about them. Could you come and introduce me to them, Jo? Oh, just one point, Sam. You will have noticed a big difference in the amount of food you use in providing for everyone. Please don't reduce any of your orders yet, though. We don't know how many more we will get, or what reserves we might need.'

'Yes. OK,' said Sam, and with that, they all dispersed.

Later, back in the office and discussing the two new admissions, Jo asked Stella how she found them.

'Quiet, more than anything,' she said. 'They both answered my questions, but only in single words. I didn't find out anything more than the information we have got and that you have told me. What I noticed above all was how lethargic they both were. While I was talking to them, each of them lay back on their pillows. I suppose it's natural that they would be quiet, coming to a new place and being not sure of what's going to happen, but John kept repeating how tired he felt. He said he felt better than he had been, because he had lost that horrible heavy feeling that he'd had in his chest, but he could not be bothered to sit up in bed and do anything.'

'That's what I thought,' said Jo. 'Well, the hospital sent a supply of their medication, so apart from that, let's give them the quiet they want.'

The routine continued. Stella and Jo had felt some release from their obligations now that Dennis, Matt, Ella and Barbara had moved out, but they seemed as busy as ever, especially at meal-times, when they left the dining room to Nicky and took food and drink upstairs to John and Eleanor and to Maggie in No. 5.

The intermediates had been admitted on Friday 5th June, and on the Saturday and Sunday, relatives of both of them rang to ask about visiting arrangements. Stella and Jo told them there was no visiting, and noticed that each of them received lengthy phone calls in their rooms. Stella wondered why, if they were so keen to talk to them, they could not have them in their homes yet, but, as Jo said, there could be any number of reasons why not.

Monday June 8th was a quiet day. The guests who wanted to do jigsaws had all they needed got out of the cupboard and provided for them after lunch. At the end of the afternoon, Sam provided his usual warm soup and then a cold supper of pasta salad. Stella took the cold part of the meal up to John and Eleanor, while Jo took a helping to Maggie. Once everything had been cleared away and the guests had gone back to their rooms to watch TV, leaving the kitchen lounge television to Sam and Nicky, it was the end of an ordinary day and everyone went to bed.

Next morning at ten to seven, Stella went to give John and Eleanor their metformin tablets. She visited Eleanor first. She was slow to rouse, but soon became more friendly than she had been over the weekend. She took her tablet without any demur, got out of bed with Stella's encouragement and accepted her help to get to the door of the en-suite, though she said she thought she could manage the toilet on her own. Stella left her smiling and said she would come back to help her with washing in just a few minutes.

When Stella knocked and opened John's door, however, there was no answer and so she switched on the light at the door. What she saw was like a kick to the heart. Momentarily she had noticed the silence before she put on the light. Now she saw the stillness. She approached John with a sinking heart as she looked at the calm and pallid serenity she had seen so many times before. John was propped up on his pillows but leaning back at about thirty degrees. His hands and arms were resting outside the duvet, motionless like the rest of him. Stella grasped his hand: it was not icy cold, but was chilled. She felt everywhere, on his face, jaw, neck and wrist, where there should have been a pulse. Nothing.

Stella reached across him to press the button which activated her pager and which she hoped would also sound on Jo's pager and bring her to the room. She pulled down the duvet and top sheet, tore open John's pyjama jacket, and began CPR. Every feeling she had told her it was pointless, but she knew she had to do it on John's lifeless body until Jo came.

Jo was there in five minutes. As she pushed open the door, she was a bit breathless from running up the stairs, but when she saw what Stella was doing, she was instantly aware of every aspect of the situation.

'I'll take over,' she said. She jumped on the bed as Stella gave way without needing to say anything. Jo knelt astride John's body and began the CPR. 'How long have you been doing it?'

'Only about five or six minutes,' said Stella. 'I knew you'd come.'

'Well, I'll have to do it for the same time,' said Jo.

They both watched John's face without speaking and with a stoical acceptance of the inevitable. Jo's initial burst of energy soon subsided.

'There's no point in wasting an ambulance with a 999 call,' said Jo.

'I agree,' said Stella, 'and that's what the hospital will say when I phone them. They'll send Borrett's now, before they get busy with anything else, and when they take him back to the morgue, one of their doctors will look at him and immediately sign the certificate, but I expect there will also be a post mortem.'

'It won't go down in the hospital's records as a Covid death,' said Jo in a subdued tone.

'That was the whole point in the first place,' muttered Stella. 'They knew.'

Borrett's were some time in coming, and Nicky had finished serving, had helped in the kitchen, had her own breakfast, and had come through into the laundry lounge. She had just folded up her own bedclothes and was standing up her foam bed in the corner when she noticed the black van come in at the Woodside Avenue entrance and drive slowly to the laundry door.

She gave a little start and moved over to the window to sit down and watch. At the same time, Stella came down the stairs, closed the door from the kitchen lounge and came through the laundry lounge to take the men through and back up the stairs to John's room. Nicky and her Dad saw each other and made a kissing gesture with their lips as he passed by. She stayed in the same position for his return journey with the blanket-covered stretcher. They exchanged looks full of emotional meaning. After they had gone, Nicky drew the sleeve of her blouse quickly across her eyes. Her eyes stung and her throat hurt. She was not there to see her father do the same thing with the sleeve of his jumper when he sat down in the van ready to drive away.

Later on that same day, Eleanor's family decided that they had now made satisfactory arrangements to receive her at their home, and so there was another double journey across the same lounge, but this time by paramedics carrying Eleanor on a stretcher. After Eleanor's personal belongings had been loaded in as well, Stella was able to collect both sets of bedding and take them down to Maggie in the laundry, sanitise both rooms and then send both invoices off to the hospital trust.

After that terrible Tuesday, Stella hoped that now there would be some respite from the physical and emotional blows that Woodside Lodge seemed to be constantly suffering. Being in touch by telephone with other colleagues in the care home business, she was aware that not many care homes were affected by the same degree of distress. They were losing residents in the course of natural events, and they had isolated, not accepting admissions, but they did not experience the same anguish that Woodside was doing.

There was then a little respite, but only until the end of the week, Friday 12th June. Since Ella had gone into hospital on 2nd June, May and June between them had decided that, because Stella and Jo were so busy looking after everyone when they had only Nicky to help them, they would do what they could to help. The only way they could do so, it seemed, was with the afternoon teas. When they had had such a busy morning and lunchtime each day, said May to June, it would be good for them to rest upstairs during the afternoon without having to run around after everyone with the tea trolley. Stella much appreciated their thoughtfulness, especially as they were among the fittest of the guests, and so from the day they had seen Ella taken away, they considered themselves on "afternoon tea duty". Always busy, helpful and friendly, they relished it. Usually, during the time they were buzzing about, the car park was busy. Increasingly, being denied any visiting, most relatives now came to the outside window of the laundry lounge and spent minutes touching it while the guests did the same from the inside. For the moment, there was no provision at the Lodge for meeting inside with a glass partition, but that would also mean an entrance and exit unused by anyone else. Stella was thinking about it.

During the following week, though, May realised that June was leaving much of the work to her, and when she asked June about it, she admitted feeling a bit "fed up" with doing it every afternoon, even if there were fewer people than there used to be. May had always been the more lively and busy of the two, and she was happy, but then noticed that June had also lost her cheerfulness and friendliness. On the Thursday, June complained, but only to May, about the lunch. May had really enjoyed it: thin pork chops, potatoes, carrots and broccoli, with apple pie and custard to follow. 'What more could you want?' she asked June. 'It was tasty, varied and there was plenty of it.'

'I didn't think it was tasty,' June replied in a very sulky manner. 'In fact, I couldn't taste it at all and I only ate half of it. That toad-in-the-hole he gave us the day before, and that chicken with salad the day before that, I couldn't taste them. Might as well have been eating cardboard. Horrible.'

'You seem to be so grumpy these days, June.' May changed the subject slightly. 'It's not like you. Do you feel alright?'

'Yeah. I'm OK. Just a bit worn out with all this walking about. It makes me tired all the time. I think I'll go and lie down and read a book in my room.'

May didn't like to argue with June, and so just got on with what she had promised to do. When she went up to the office to fetch the empty teapot Stella and Jo had used (they always used and cleaned their own cups), Jo was quick to notice her listless manner. 'Are you alright, May?' she asked.

'Yes, thank you,' May answered, but Stella's suspicion did not go away.

'Is June alright, too?' Stella asked. 'We haven't seen much of her the last few days. It always seems to be you collecting the tea things.'

May did not want to criticise or be disloyal to June. She was her best friend and she should support her. 'She's OK. She feels a bit tired and she was moaning about the lunch, but she's alright and she's gone for a lie-down.'

'Right. Thanks, May. Be careful with that tray.'

May made an efficient exit, and that was the end of the conversation.

'I've got a feeling about this, Jo,' said Stella as soon as she had gone. 'It's not usually like this with those two. They're usually both full of bounce.'

'Just gone off this idea of doing the tea,' suggested Jo.

'M'm. I'm not convinced. When things change, be watchful,' said Stella. 'I think I'll go and call on June in her room. I'll take a thermometer and think of an excuse to take her temperature. I'll tell her it's just routine, that I'm calling on everybody.'

She returned a few minutes later. Jo had moved into the room next door, usually the sitting room, and now Jo's bedsit as well. Stella found her. 'Thirty-eight. Nothing to worry about,' said Stella. 'It's a warm day, and she has been walking about.'

When Stella went down to give Sam and Nicky a hand with the soup that preceded the cold supper, she noticed June had stayed in her room. When she asked May if she knew where June was, she just shrugged.

At the first opportunity, Stella left the dining room and walked to June's room, at No. 17 almost the furthest one round. She found June lying on her bed, and she agreed to have some soup but nothing to eat. 'Just a small slice of Bakewell tart?' Stella asked.

'Ugh!' June pulled a face. 'No thank you. It'll be the same as most of Sam's meals are these days. The middle bit might as well be sawdust. Don't want any.'

Stella knew that it was uncharacteristic of June to be so offhand and a bit uncouth about Sam's cooking. She asked a few more questions about other subjects and was met by the same response and a complaint that June felt too tired to bother going to the dining room.

When supper was over, and everything had been cleared away and washed and Sam had everything prepared for Friday's breakfast, Stella returned to June's room. Sure enough, she was still resting on the bed, lying back against the pillows. She had dozed off while reading her book, but stirred and then fully woke up when Stella made enough noise to rouse her. Stella explained to June that she was concerned about her tiredness and wanted to check her oxygen levels.

'Ninety three,' she muttered, when she had taken the reading, and thanked June. 'Promise me you'll get a good night's sleep now, and I'll come and check you over again first thing in the morning.' Stella was still uneasy about her and yet she thought that she didn't qualify as an emergency. All her readings were the wrong side of normal, but this tiredness and lack of good humour were worrying. The person who knew her best, May, was also uneasy. Stella had already told her not to bother with the tea tomorrow. She, Stella, would do it.

On Friday morning, the oxygen level had dropped further, but her temperature was the same and she felt no tiredness. She had, though, coughed quite a lot during the night. Stella decided not to take any risks, and at 8 am phoned Dr Attwood. If Brookfields was bursting at the seams, that was not her problem. The doctor seemed never to physically examine patients any more, and so Stella thought she would trade on his goodwill before the day got busy. She gave him the information she had and suggested he got her admitted to hospital. He was not too keen, and the conversation had many long, silent pauses, but in the end he agreed. By a coincidence, June had quite a long spell of coughing when Stella was able to turn her attention back to her.

The ambulance came just after breakfast had been finished with. The visit was quite unobtrusive. Some guests were still lingering over a final cup of tea. Room 17 was one of the most distant ones, and so Jo, dressed again in her full PPE, could go and direct the ambulance round to the far door.

The one person who did not fail to notice it, though, was May, who went rushing upstairs to find Stella. As Jo was with June and the paramedics, Stella was in the office. May had worked herself up into quite an emotional state.

'Oh Stella, what's the matter?' May burst out. 'I haven't seen June this morning, but she was only tired yesterday, that was all. I know she was a bit rude, and usually she isn't, but that doesn't matter. You know she's my friend, and I love her. What is it? What is it?' She actually lunged towards Stella, wanting to embrace, as she had done before this pandemic had changed everything, but Stella kept her composure and stepped backwards.

'We must distance, May,' she said, 'but it's alright. June has just gone to the hospital for some more tests, because I'm concerned about all her tiredness, and I'm taking precautions. It's alright, May. I'm just playing safe.' There was not the aggression and the shouting and the threats that Stella had had to put up with from Barbara when Ella was taken away. May was not like that. Stella thought how sweet she was as she stood in front of her, tearful and trembling. She would not be reassured. Then she threw both arms round her own waist, in the absence of any comfort from Stella. She gave a little choking simper, and then turned, went out and rushed down the stairs. She did not stop rushing or simpering until she got to her own room, No. 13, in the far corridor. Then she threw herself on her bed and sobbed uncontrollably.

Stella thought it was best to let her go and be on her own for a while. She was inconsolable at present. She would go and visit her later. She went through into the sitting room and sat for a short while. Her heart was heavy. The Lodge, this place into which she had poured her life and soul, seemed suddenly full of turmoil and pain.

About fifteen minutes later, Brookfields hospital phoned soon after they had admitted June. Stella had anticipated this, and had taken her records from the filing cabinet so that she could read over the phone all the updated part that the hospital would need to know. After she had finished doing that, there was a pause and then the person at the other end calmly announced that June had tested positive for Covid-19 and was, as they were speaking, being moved into the Covid ward. Stella drew a quick breath and closed her eyes. Yet another one of her guests had caught the virus. Without testing equipment of her own, which she had ordered but not yet received, Stella was at a loss as to how to deal with it.

The phone rang again an hour later. It was the hospital again, regretting to inform her that two of her residents, Ella and Matt, admitted on the 2nd and 4th of June, had both died early that morning. She was numbed by the shock. Her world was closing down. Life was being smothered by a suffocating black blanket.

Even more was to come. After another half an hour, the phone rang again. 'Good-day to you , Mrs Holden.' The voice at the other end was suave, fluent and well-spoken. 'Do you remember me, Jack Scott? I spoke to you about three months ago when I visited my Aunt May, whom I pay for as one of your residents. I'm her next of kin as she's a widow with no family of her own. Do you remember? I asked if she might come off the Levoxyl, which she takes for thyroid deficiency. She had been depressed and anxious before she came to Woodside Lodge, but as soon as she arrived, she made a great friend of another of your residents, June, and was suddenly happy, much more outgoing and not in need of that drug any more. Do you remember?'

'Yes. I do remember your visit, Mr Scott. We did withdraw her from Levoxyl after some more tests with Dr Attwood, who is the GP who looks after us. She has remained happy ever since, Mr Scott, full of energy, always "on the go", and everybody's friend.'

'But when she phoned me a short time ago, she seemed very upset because this friend of hers, June, has been taken away to hospital. Is that true, Miss Holden?'

Stella's spirits sank again. There was only one policy at times like this and that was to be absolutely truthful and tell the caller what they wanted to know, provided no-one else was jeopardised by that. 'Yes. That's so, Mr Scott.'

'She went on to say that June had been out of sorts lately, and that you thought that June had caught the coronavirus, and that was why you had sent her to hospital. Is that true, as well, Miss Holden?'

'Yes,' said Stella in a flat, resigned tone. 'That is what I thought and I thought the safest thing, for her and for the people who live in this home, was to send her for tests and treatment at the hospital. A short time ago, the hospital rang to say that she had tested positive for Covid-19, and I am doubtful if she will ever return here. May will not be allowed to visit her in hospital.'

'Well, she is so upset,' resumed Jack Scott, 'that, now that she is not taking any medication, it will be best if my wife and I have her here with us, so that we can perhaps keep her spirits up.'

'Righto. If that's what you want,' said Stella. There was nothing to argue about.

'OK, then. It's a fairly long drive, but if you can have May and all her possessions packed and ready by about half-past four, I can see you then. Is that alright?'

'Yes,' said Stella, quite tonelessly. She wondered how much more she could take. Now she had to phone the next of kin of Matt and Ella.

Chapter 12

It was late on Friday evening. Jo had just finished doing a quick tour of the building and the corridors, and went into the sitting room to find Stella drooped in an armchair.

'Oh, come on, Stella. If you don't buck up and keep going, how do you expect everyone else to manage? Everything seems OK, and most people have already gone to bed.'

Stella was cradling a warm cup of Ovaltine into which she was peering, as if it was a crystal ball. 'Oh, sorry, Jo, but my word, I'm glad to see you. I really want someone to talk to. I'm sick of the same old things going round and round in my head.'

'What sort of things are those, then, Stella?' asked Jo. She had gone over to the small draining board in the corner of the sitting room and began to make herself a cup of Ovaltine, too. 'What's on your mind?'

'Some pretty dark things,' said Stella, slowly. 'I think we're sinking, Jo.'

Jo stopped as she walked across to the other armchair. 'That's a bit dramatic, Stella. What is it?'

'The hospital phoned this morning to say that June had tested positive for Covid. If we include John and Eleanor, that makes seven people from this care home who to our knowledge have suffered from Covid. Let me just go through them. We started with Dennis and Maggie, then Ella, Matt and June. Not only that, Jo, but over the last three months of lockdown, four of our original guests are now dead. There was Martin first, and then Dennis, Matt and Ella. What happens to June remains to be seen, but Barbara and May have left us. If June does not return, that makes seven that we've lost in those three months.'

The bubbling energy with which Jo had come into the room had subsided, and as she settled comfortably into the armchair with her own warm drink, she was drawn into Stella's mood of despondency. She could not argue with the facts. 'But it's no good just wallowing in soggy feelings, Stella,' she said. 'We just need to think what we can do about things.'

'That's difficult, Jo. Covid has got in here, and we don't know how. The one thing they know about this virus is that it is transmitted between people, but we are taking all the precautions I can think of. We wash everything including ourselves. We clean everything and sanitise everything. We reasonably keep our distance although in a home like this you can't strictly keep your full two-metre distance and we are what they call "a bubble". If anyone becomes ill, they are isolated in their own unit where they have everything they need and only one person, wearing full protective gear, goes in and out for food, drink and medication. We have a doctor's advice and a hospital on hand. What more can we do? Only isolate ourselves from the outside world, and we've been doing that.'

'Can we learn from anyone else? What is it like for other care homes, Stella? Do you know?'

'I'm in touch with a few, mostly friends of mine, and most of them say they are clear of it and are totally isolating themselves to make sure they stay that way. If they lose one of their residents, they won't admit anyone else under any circumstances, and so there's no contact with anyone else at all.'

'We could have more support technically.' Jo knew that was a weak argument, and Stella couldn't do anything about the shortcomings.

'We keep on being told we're going to get testing equipment,' said Stella, 'but it never comes, and I was sure the bit we had one time didn't work. All we've had to go on is the symptoms. The same applies to PPE. Some of the stuff we've had sent to us was so sub-standard we might as well not have had it and I threw it away. At least we have enough for the staff to wear when necessary, but that only amounts to you and me, not Sam and Nicky. What would I do without them, bless 'em?' She paused for a short time. 'So what's to do?'

'We just soldier on, I suppose, Stella. I'll always be here to support you.'

'I know you will.' Stella looked up into Jo's face with all the feelings she had. 'But now that we are down to eleven out of the original eighteen, we are running at a loss. There's no point in going on and on until all the accounts go down to nothing and then into the red.'

'Are you taking in any more intermediates?'

'I'm expecting to have more offered any day, but I feel guilty about that, Jo. The hospital knows that the people they send have already succumbed to the virus and will soon be gone, or can go back to their relatives. They are just another statistic that won't appear on their lists of deaths from the virus.'

'That's bitter.'

'That's how I feel, Jo, and the reason I feel guilty is that I have a sense of responsibility for everyone else who is here and has not been ill. It's not only you, Sam and Nicky, but what about Vic, Jane and Margery, Lorna and Chris and half a dozen others? Do we just wait for the attack? The intermediates bring the cursed thing in, and any financial help is only temporary. The more I have, the more danger there is, because they'll be untested.'

'Yes. I see what you mean,' said Jo. 'Will you advertise anymore?'

'The same feeling of guilt will still apply,' said Stella, 'and, in any case, no-one wants to send their relative into a home in the present circumstances. As I said, those that I know won't have any more anyway.'

'Yes. There doesn't seem to be any option whichever way you look,' said Jo.

'It makes me laugh when the Department of Health puts out statements like that one yesterday: '60% of care homes have avoided infection,' he said, and on the same day a "Newsnight" programme showed that when a whole lot of people had a testing kit in their homes, nearly all of them tested positive and yet had no symptoms. So, is this the way the virus sometimes behaves, or is it a poor test that gave false readings? How does anybody know? That app. trialled in the Isle of Wight last week, a "world beater" the PM said, has been found to be so unreliable it can't be used. "We have beaten the virus," the Minister said yesterday. What? Beaten the virus, on a day when 200 people died, 1200 new infections were reported, and the total death toll is now 42,288. What do they think we are? Stupid?'

There was another pause, and both ladies finished their drinks and sat peering into the bottoms of the mugs. Jo did not want to take the conversation forward any further; it would be so hurtful to Stella.

'As I said,' Stella resumed, 'the situation is that we are sinking. There's no point in ignoring it, and I have to decide, with advice from you if necessary, what to do about it. I have poured my life and soul into this place. It's my life and has been for about fifteen years now. I always thought my parents would have been pleased and proud of what I've done with the home they gave me, and now it's come to this.

'I'll still have the building and the land when everything else has gone. I don't want the market value or the money for it. What would I do living on my own in a small flat? I've still got so much to give, and I'll have to think of some other way that I can use the property to serve my fellow human beings. Still, I suppose it's not my fault, and I do feel grateful for what you, Maggie, Sam and

Nicky have done. I'll try to give you some reward at the end, but, although I will be cutting costs and trying not to go into the red, it will be expensive for me with redundancy pay to give everyone, and making sure the present residents are looked after when the time comes.'

Jo had to ask: 'You just mentioned "the end" and "when the time comes", Stella. What do you have in mind?'

'There's no point in burying my head in the sand, Jo, and discretion really is the better part of valour when it comes down to it. Her voice shook when she had to say it. Strong and experienced a nurse and a woman as she was, her throat nearly closed with emotion. 'I'll have to close and arrange for everyone to go.' The tears stung, as she picked up the mugs, dashed over to the sink and kept her back to Jo. Jo needed every bit of her training and experience to stop herself going and putting her arms round her.

'I'd better go to bed, now, Jo. See you in the morning.'

There was the usual busy morning the next day, Saturday 13th June. At half-past six, Stella, who hadn't slept much during the night, went along the rooms in both corridors, knocking on doors and calling "Good morning" eleven times, although her real purpose was to note whether there was an answer at all. Almost none of them needed any help with getting out of bed, washing or attending the toilet, but Stella usually looked in on Margery as being the most likely.

Then Jo did the round with medication, and gave Margery and Mick their warfarin, but there was now no-one left who took beta-blockers. Lew and Lorna were the only ones taking the metformin tablets, now that June had gone to the hospital. Chris and Marsha looked after themselves with their inhalers, preventers and relievers, and Jane and Marsha still needed their Naproxen. The medication didn't take anywhere near as long these days, and there was no-one left who was awkward about it.

Breakfast tended to be a meal that everyone lingered over these days, especially the tea and toast at the end. There was now no-one who could not go to the dining room. As soon as it had been cleared away and the staff had had theirs, the three ladies did another tour of the eleven occupied rooms, armed with hand-vacs, dustpans and brushes, bin-bags for what rubbish there was, and buckets of warm water to clean the toilets and washbasins.

This was the usual morning routine, and the staff met for a cup of coffee in the office at eleven. What was unusual, though, was that Stella was careful to insist that Sam, Nicky and Maggie attended on this Saturday, as well as Jo. Sam grumbled a bit, saying that he didn't usually attend, and could spare only a few minutes because he had lunch to prepare and cook.

Stella wasted no time once they had all assembled, and when she told them what she had to do in the near future, Sam soon saw why they all had to be there. She explained the situation briefly, very much as she and Jo had discussed it the evening before. She was listened to in silence and she went on to say that once someone had made up their mind about matters like this, it was best to get it done as quickly as possible. Therefore, she was aiming to close Woodside Lodge in one month's time, about the middle of July, provided that she could make provision for all the guests, that is, if their families could take them back or make other arrangements, or if another care home could take them, although that seemed most unlikely at the moment. She also said that she was sure that Sam, Nicky and Maggie would quickly get jobs elsewhere, especially with the excellent references she would give them all. Their last pay cheque would be the end of July, to give them more than a month's notice and she would pay severance pay as soon as the accountant had worked it out. She told Sam, especially, that the Government was starting a so-called "Eat out to help out" scheme to help the catering industry in August, and she advised him to get his feet under someone's table as soon as possible.

Nicky was the first one to speak: 'But where am I going to live, Stella? she asked. 'Can I stay on and live here with you for a while? Sam and Maggie have both got their empty flats to go back to, and Jo has her house, but I can't go and endanger everyone in my family by moving in with them again until I have isolated for at least two weeks.'

'Yes, of course you can stay here, Nicky, until you are able to move out. I'll be glad of your company, and I should guess that Jo won't be in a hurry to go back to her empty house.'

'No. I'd like to stay here as well if I may, Stella, until Ken comes back home again from his present voyage. I won't be in a hurry to get another job.'

'Yes. That will be alright, Jo. You know it will.'

With that, everyone gathered up whatever they had brought with them, and walked out quietly, to go and think over these matters.

For the rest of the morning and over lunchtime, Sam, Nicky, Maggie and Jo went quietly about their tasks. They were wondering what the future held. They had been taken almost unawares, surprised and shocked by the suddenness of it, the speed of events.

Only Stella knew it was coming. It had been a terrible week: John, Ella and Matt dead, Barbara, June and May gone. Stella must have been watching and waiting. Each of them wondered what she must have been thinking and feeling. Then she had told them so quickly and calmly, as if she was talking about a minor incident of the day before. But this was the end of everything. Everyone needed time to take it in.

Stella had a feeling of unreality. It was almost as if it was taking place at a distance, in a dream. She was absolutely confident, though, that she had made the right decision. She had done all she could. It was inevitable.

She sat with her cup of tea after lunch with Jo. 'Nothing more to be said, Jo. I'll get in touch with all the next of kin people this afternoon. They'll be at home on a Saturday while lockdown is on. Then they'll think about it, consult the rest of the family, and mull it over on Sunday. I'll try to impress on them the urgency of closing down. I'll tell them that no other home will take them, and that, as far as I know, is absolutely true. I think the best way to get them to act is to frighten them with Covid. I'll tell them it's a lethal presence in this building, and their loved one is in the direct line of fire.'

Jo sat wordlessly, silently, like the others.

'Right then, Jo. Would you hold the fort for a couple of hours? I would like to do what I did last Friday afternoon, slip out with no-one seeing me and walk in the wood again, alone with my thoughts.'

'Yes. OK,' said Jo. 'It must be heavy on your mind.'

'Thanks, Jo.' And Stella set off.

She had walked in the wood only once since lockdown. That was only last Friday, although six days was beginning to feel like a lifetime ago. But she did that walk quite often before lockdown, always on her own, because it was mental therapy she needed rather than physical exercise. Indeed, she had done it most of her life, while her parents were alive and before Woodside Lodge was hers and was a care home. Whenever she had been under any stress, the greenness and the naturalness and the fresh air soothed her mind and revived her spirits. Cords of tension loosened, and the gnawing acid of aggression left her. Especially at this time of the year, late Spring and early summer, she liked to close her eyes, open her ears and immerse herself in the natural world. At the end of an hour's walk there, she used to feel that she had had an emotional bath.

Stella quickly reached the boundary of the Woodside Lodge grounds, and was soon through the end gate and into the middle part of the wood dominated by coppices of hazels, where she had sat last Friday. She passed this point and travelled on to the further fringes of the wood, where there were hawthorns, holly and elderberry bushes.

Now, the blackthorn and hawthorn were in full leaf, working to produce the purple sloes and red haws of the autumn ahead. In the pasture that lay between the more sparse trees and bushes grew foxgloves, cowslips, teasels, primroses, buttercups, clover and dog violets, all harbouring a rich and diverse harvest for blackbird and starling, chaffinch and greenfinch. Even the thistles fed the goldfinches and linnets.

Stella closed her eyes and felt the peace and happiness penetrating every part of her mind and spirit. She could hear the fizzing, buzzing and whizzing of insects everywhere. Life was being lived with all its natural energy. The sights and sounds of the birds filled her senses as they scurried and scuttled about on the endless cycle of displaying, mating and feeding. The tiny wrens were especially loud, lurking at the foot of the tangled, chunky bushes as they sang their hearts out to the world about them. By contrast, the willow warblers contributed the sweetness of their falling cadences. There was the pulsating rise and fall of the chiffchaff and the fluid trills of the robin, shaken out at random on the breeze. The bold, clear, repetitive phrases of the song thrush shouted from the very top of bush or tree, contrasted with the full-throated, rich melodies of the blackbird. Stella sat on a wooden seat and, still with closed eyes, she yielded to the enfolding peace of the moment. The living beauty of it all healed her wounded soul.

Finally, Stella got up from the seat and walked back the way she had come. What did it all matter? She would not starve. She had more money than most other people in the world.

Having turned, she was walking back eastwards. She felt the sunshine warm on her shoulders and back. It felt like a warm caress. The sun was the source of all earthly energy. It was indifferent to all human passion, aspirations and feelings. It shone on everyone and everything, just and unjust, deserving and undeserving. All that mattered was that great spectacle of life that she had just soaked up on the edge of the wood.

As she walked across the green coolness of the lawns and approached the Lodge, a few spots of rain began to fall softly on her hair and shoulders. She looked at the sky beyond the building and saw the pale colours of a fresh rainbow.

***